7th Heaven

MATT'S STORY

Based on the hit TV series
created by Brenda Hampton

Based on teleplays and stories
by Brenda Hampton and Ron Darien

Random House  New York

Library of Congress Catalog Card Number: 99-64376
ISBN: 0-375-80333-5

Printed in the United States of America
November 1999
10 9 8 7 6 5 4 3 2 1

RANDOM HOUSE and colophon are registered trademarks
of Random House, Inc.

ONE

"I can't believe you dragged me out to that stupid movie!" Matt Camden's date cried. "And tonight, of all nights!"

Shana's voice was so filled with anger that it froze Matt in his tracks.

"I don't think so," Matt protested. "It was *your* idea to go out."

"Why would I want to go to a movie?" Shana replied. "*I'm* the one with the psychology test—"

"Which you said you'd studied for," Matt interrupted.

"I should never have listened to you," Shana said. "I should have stayed home and studied, like I'd planned to do all along."

"Whatever happened to, 'Oh, Matt, I

feel so trapped in this teeny, tiny apartment. Can't we go out for just a little while?"

Shana's eyes narrowed. "You've got a lot of nerve, Camden," she said.

"What have I said that wasn't true?" Matt demanded.

"All right! I do admit that I said I felt cooped up," Shana relented. "But that's only because we're always using my apartment as a study hall."

"You have a great apartment," Matt said.

"Yeah." Shana nodded. "Great for *you!* When you come over, you're a visitor."

"Well," Matt said, "we could go to my house. And while we're there, we could listen to my twin baby brothers crying constantly as we try to discuss Freud over all the noise!"

Shana sighed. "You always have a defense, don't you?"

"Defense?" Matt said. "But *I* didn't do anything wrong."

"Then it's my fault?" Shana retorted.

"Nothing's anybody's fault," Matt insisted. "Why do you want to fight?"

"Because I'm tired of it all, Matt," Shana replied.

"All what?" he said. "Are you tired of *me?*"

"I'm certainly tired of your selfish behavior," Shana shot back.

"*Selfish?*" Matt cried. "I can't believe I'm hearing this. I was just trying to make you happy."

"Are you saying you were *handling* me?" Shana demanded.

Matt paused before answering. "Yeah," he said finally. "Only I should have handled you better."

Shana's face was livid with rage. She took two steps away from Matt.

"I'm an *adult!*" she shouted. "I don't need *you* to make me study. You're not my big brother."

"Sometimes you *do* need handling," Matt said simply.

"Why, you—you—you...!" Shana stammered, searching for just the right insult.

"Adult?" Matt offered, raising one eyebrow.

"No," Shana said. "Definitely *not* an adult."

"What's *that* supposed to mean?"

"An adult doesn't live with his parents," Shana said. "An adult doesn't live with all his little brothers and sisters. An adult has his own apartment, like I do."

"And an adult *finds* her own apartment," Matt countered. "She doesn't have her boyfriend's father find it for her."

"Your father helped me find my place when things were bad with my family," Shana argued. "But I pay the rent. *All* of it!"

"Look, Shana, it's still early," Matt said reasonably. "Why don't we go back to your place and do some studying? I'm sure hitting the books will convince you that you're ready for your test."

"Oh, I'm ready, all right," Shana said, crossing her arms. "Ready to get on with my life! Without *you!*"

"Come on, Shana," Matt urged, moving toward her. "Take it easy."

He tried to gather her into his arms, but she pushed him away.

"I'm ready to date an adult," she said. "Someone with an actual plan for the future!"

"Shana—" Matt's tone was pleading, but Shana was already heading across Crawford College's green at a rapid pace.

"Call me when you've grown up," she called over her shoulder.

"Shana, come back," Matt pleaded. "At

least let me drive you home."

"I can walk," Shana said without turning.

"I'll call you tomorrow," Matt said.

But Shana walked on as if she hadn't heard him.

Almost immediately, Matt's anger turned ito regret. He wanted to run after her, but his pride got in the way.

"Have it your way!" Matt yelled. "There are plenty of other women who would *love* to date a warm, considerate guy like me."

With a toss of his long brown hair, Matt turned—and froze.

Two female graduate students had come out of Wylie Hall just in time to witness the argument with Shana.

The young woman giggled.

"Anybody want a date with a warm, considerate guy?" Matt quipped to cover his embarrassment.

"Sorry, kid," one of the students replied with a sly smile. "I like men, not boys…and I hear you don't even have your own apartment."

Matt winced. He didn't hear the flirting tone of the young woman's voice—only her insulting words.

"Better run home to your mommy," the other student chimed in. "I'm sure she turned down the sheets for you."

The two young women exploded in gales of laughter and walked away. But their laughter burned Matt's ears long after they were gone.

Ruthie was still awake when Matt got home. She greeted him at the door.

"Hey, Ruthie," Matt said, stepping past his little sister and giving her head a rub.

Ruthie trailed him as he crossed the kitchen. She cocked her head when he lifted the phone.

"Who are you calling?" she asked. "It's late."

Matt heard Lucy's voice on the receiver. She was talking to Jordan on the other extension. Matt quickly hung up.

"I guess I'm not calling anybody," he replied. "The line is busy. As usual."

He looked down at Ruthie. "Did anybody call tonight?"

"Jordan called Lucy," Ruthie said.

"I mean, did anybody call *me*?"

Ruthie shrugged.

"Try to remember, Ruthie," Matt pleaded. "It's really important."

"I don't know if anybody called you," Ruthie said after careful consideration. "But I'll definitely keep an ear open."

"Thanks." Matt patted her shoulder.

As he tried to raid the refrigerator, Ruthie thrust a book under his nose.

"Read me a story," she demanded.

Matt carried a carton of milk to the table and poured out two glasses. He handed one to Ruthie and took a sip from the other. Then he sat down, and Ruthie hopped onto his lap.

The book was a thick volume filled with all the storybook classics.

"Which one do you want to hear?" he asked.

Ruthie pointed to her favorite. Matt sighed. He'd read this story so many times he knew it by heart.

"Once upon a time..." Matt began.

"I've never met Jimmy Moon," Jordan said to Lucy. "But I've heard that he's kind of a jerk. Hangs out with the wrong crowd."

"Jimmy?" Lucy said, surprised. "He's actually a pretty nice guy. It just didn't work out between us, that's all."

"Hmm," Jordan said.

Lucy felt a sudden jolt of apprehension.

"Just what *did* you hear about Jimmy?" she asked, trying to sound casual.

Jordan was silent.

"Well?" Lucy said.

"I just didn't think Jimmy Moon was your type, that's all," Jordan said finally.

"Well, maybe you just don't know me as well as you think," Lucy said teasingly.

"Forget I said anything." Jordan sighed. "I don't like to talk about stuff like that."

"Stuff like *what?*" Lucy pressed. "You brought it up. Now you've got to come clean! What's wrong with Jimmy?"

"Let's just drop it, okay?" Jordan was firm.

Lucy was unwilling to drop the subject, though. Jordan's words had alarmed her. But when she tried again to find out what he meant, Jordan said good-bye and hung up.

Lucy put the phone down. Her mind was in turmoil.

What's up with my ex-boyfriend? she wondered.

"I'm going to miss having you around," Mrs. Camden sighed. "But I guess all things must pass."

As she spoke, Mrs. Camden was feeding David. His twin, Samuel, slept soundly in his crib.

Rev. Camden gave his wife's shoulders a squeeze. "That's nice to hear," he said with a smile. "But family leave is over as of tomorrow. I'll be returning to my church work full-time."

Mrs. Camden smiled at the baby in her arms. "We've been selfish to keep Daddy away from his work, haven't we, my little precious David?"

"We've still got a few hours left," Rev. Camden said.

"Then let's make the most of them," Mrs. Camden replied.

Mary muted the television and faced her brother, who'd been hovering around her for the last half hour.

"Okay, Simon. What's so important that I have to miss the end of the game to talk to you?" Mary demanded.

"Baseball," Simon replied.

"Baseball?" Mary said, confused.

"I'm going for catcher." Simon made the announcement with dramatic flair.

"What does that have to do with me?" Mary asked.

"I need your help," Simon said. "Matt's

always at school. And Dad's always with Mom, who's—"

"Always with the twins," Mary finished. "Get on with it."

"I want you to help me practice tomorrow. Just throw me some balls, maybe give me some tips."

Mary smiled. "Why would you ever think of asking Matt, anyway? He can't pitch, he can't hit."

"Well, I know you're the best, but I just thought…" Simon's voice trailed off.

"I'm good and you know it. And I know how the coach thinks. He used to coach me, but I doubt he'd remember."

"Then you *can* help?" Simon said hopefully.

"Oil up your glove and we'll give it a go in the morning," Mary promised.

Simon slapped his sister's hand. "Thanks!"

"But right now I want to watch the rest of this game. Okay?"

"Sure," Simon said. "I'm out of here."

Simon headed out to the garage to find oil for his glove.

"With my talent, and Mary's brand-name athletic reputation, I'm as good as on that team already!"

* * *

Early the next morning, Rev. Camden was in the kitchen, hard at work making bologna sandwiches for the kids' school lunches. Kitchen work had never been one of his strong suits, and even making a simple sandwich called for an undue amount of concentration on Rev. Camden's part.

Added to that was his apprehension about his first day back at the church after his long leave. He thought he'd noticed some tension the last time he'd spoken to Lou, one of the deacons. Rev. Camden hoped his absence hadn't put too much pressure on the deacons.

"Hey, Dad," Matt said.

"Don't distract me or I'll forget something. I have to focus on this. The key to my life right now is focus."

Matt grinned. "First-day-back jitters?"

"You could say that…"

As Matt watched in horrified fascination, his father loaded up four slices of bread with lettuce leaves. Then he added three slices of bologna to each sandwich. He came up with one extra slice of bologna, which he offered to Matt.

While Matt chewed, Rev. Camden topped each sandwich with mayonnaise, then plopped on the top piece of bread.

"*Voilà!*" Rev. Camden proclaimed. "A culinary masterpiece."

"That's nice, Dad," Matt said. "Pretty soon, you'll be giving Wolfgang Puck competition."

"So," Rev. Camden said, washing off his hands, "since I have to get to the church this morning, I won't be able to take Mary and Lucy to school."

He looked at his son. "Could you drop them off before you go to class?"

Matt frowned. "It's not exactly on the way..."

His father's disapproving stare quickly changed his mind.

"But of course I can," Matt added. "Is there anything else I can do for you?"

"Not right now," Rev. Camden replied.

While Rev. Camden wrapped the sandwiches and packed them into bags, Matt added a banana to each lunch.

"No banana for Mary," Rev. Camden said. "She likes to get her potassium from those sports drinks or something."

Matt peeled Mary's banana and ate it.

Rev. Camden glanced at the empty fruit bowl. "I guess I'd better go shopping."

Matt leaned against the counter and caught his father's eye. "I think I'm going to look into off-campus housing today," he announced.

"Can you afford it?" Rev. Camden asked, surprised.

"I saved money all summer," Matt said with a shrug.

"I thought you were going to trade in the Camaro for a new car," said Rev. Camden.

"The way I see it, a car gets me away from the house during the day," Matt replied. "But a room on campus or off gets me away from home day *and* night."

"Sounds good," Rev. Camden agreed.

"It'd be great," Matt continued. "I'd live near school, but I'd still be close to home if I ever want to visit. Or eat."

"Or do your laundry," Rev. Camden added.

Matt smiled. "Yeah. Stuff like that."

Rev. Camden patted his son's shoulder. "I'm sure you'll make the right decision," he said.

"Thanks, Dad." Matt was smiling now. It looked as if Rev. Camden had seen the logic of his argument.

Best of all, with his own place, Matt wouldn't have to listen to Shana's complaints.

Shana! I forgot! Matt reached for the phone.

"Hold up, there!" Rev. Camden commanded. "You don't have time to make any calls."

"Huh?"

"Get your brother and sisters moving," Rev. Camden said. "I've got to get ready for work, and you are all going to be late."

"I'll get right on it," Matt replied, checking the clock. "Just as soon as I make an important phone call."

Rev. Camden shook his head in despair.

Fifteen minutes later, Matt still hadn't gotten anywhere near the phone. When he first went upstairs, Mary was using it. And when Mary hung up, Lucy insisted on calling *her* friend.

Something urgent, she claimed. Life or death. *Right*.

"What could be so important?" Matt demanded. "Everybody you know is on their way to school—where *you* will be in half an hour."

Lucy dialed the phone.

Matt leaned against the door and crossed his arms. Lucy stared at him.

"What now?" Matt cried.

"Some privacy, please."

Matt headed for his parents' bedroom to use the second line, but his mother was already talking to someone.

Matt headed back down the hall, grumbling to himself. As he went by Lucy's room, he couldn't help hearing her mention her old boyfriend, Jimmy Moon.

How could conversations about ex-boyfriends be so important? he wondered.

"I'm done!" Lucy announced a few minutes later.

As Matt reached for the phone, it rang.

The call was for his father.

"Let's go!" Mary urged. "We'll be late."

Matt grabbed his books and keys and followed the others out to the car.

"There's a pay phone at the Dairy Shack," Matt announced. "We'll be stopping there first."

He pulled into the parking lot.

"Anybody got a quarter?" he asked.

Lucy produced a coin and bounced it off his head from the backseat.

*   *   *

Rev. Camden knew something was up the moment he arrived at his office at the church. Instead of holding piles of paperwork waiting for him, his desk was empty. It looked as if Lou had covered his work for him.

"That's nice," Rev. Camden said.

But it didn't feel nice. It felt...strange. It seemed that the church could get along fine without him.

"Well," he said, "there's still the weekly bulletin. Nobody does that job but me."

Just as Rev. Camden sat down at his desk and fired up his computer, the doorbell buzzed. He rose and answered the call.

"Please sit down," Rev. Camden said to the well-dressed middle-aged couple as he ushered them into his office. They eyed him nervously. Rev. Camden studied them, his panic mounting.

I should know who these people are. Why don't I recognize them?

The man wore a harried expression. His wife's face was pinched with worry.

"What can I do for you?" Rev. Camden asked.

"It's—it's just not like our son to do something—something like this," the man said, tripping over his words.

"He's actually my stepson," the woman added quickly. "But I feel like I gave birth to him—"

"That's why we're worried," the man interrupted. "It's just not like him at all."

"I love the boy," the woman continued, talking over her husband. "But I don't love what he's doing."

"He's letting his grades drop," the man said.

"He's cutting classes," the woman added.

Rev. Camden's head began to spin.

"Even worse," the man cried, "I caught him hitchhiking the other day!"

Rev. Camden nodded. "Well—"

"We don't know where he goes anymore," the woman broke in. "We don't know who his friends are."

"We thought you might have better insight into this than we do, Reverend Camden," the man said. "You have experience with troubled kids."

"And you probably know our son as well as we do," the woman added. "Probably better."

Rev. Camden squirmed with embarrassment.

"I'm sorry," he said finally. "I think I have to apologize."

The couple looked at him quizzically.

"I've got two new babies at home, and this is my first day back in the church in weeks." Rev. Camden hesitated. "I should know who you are," he continued, "even if you're new to the church, but..."

Now his visitors looked embarrassed.

"Sorry," the man sighed. "It's our fault."

"Yes," the woman added. "We don't even go to your church."

Just then, the door to Rev. Camden's private office opened.

Lou, the oldest of the church deacons, walked into the office and froze when he saw Rev. Camden. The man had never been good at hiding his emotions, and Rev. Camden could see clearly that Lou was uncomfortable to find him there.

"Lou?" Rev. Camden asked. "Is anything the matter?"

"No, no," Lou insisted. "I—I just didn't realize that you were back from paternity leave." He turned to the surprised couple. "I'm very sorry for intruding," he said. "Please forgive me."

Then he dashed off so fast that he forgot to close the door behind him. Rev.

Camden rose and pushed the door shut.

"Sorry," he told his guests. "That was one of our deacons. He has his own office, but..."

Rev. Camden quickly buried his irritation.

"I think you were about to introduce yourselves," he said.

"I'm Norma," the woman said. "And this is my husband, Fred. Fred Moon."

Rev. Camden smiled. "Moon," he said. "Your son is Jimmy Moon."

"That's right," the man said. "Jimmy is Lucy's old boyfriend. She's a very nice girl, by the way."

"Yes," the woman added. "I was sorry to see them break up."

"Well, I was, too," Rev. Camden said tactfully.

"We really need your help," Mr. Moon said.

Mrs. Moon nodded. "We think Jimmy is doing drugs," she said.

TWO

Matt's final class of the day was canceled. Before heading back to the house, he checked with the college housing office. He was determined to find an apartment.

Unfortunately, no apartments were available.

The people at the housing office were helpful enough. They even gave him the name of a realty office. But Matt knew he couldn't afford a place to live if he had to pay a broker to find it for him.

The housing office put his name on a waiting list and assured Matt they would get back to him. But only after they got back to several hundred other people first.

The list, it appeared, was a long one.

One of Matt's classmates, a girl named

Pamela Hensleigh, suggested he try the campus bulletin boards. He checked a few, but all he saw was ads for Zen workshops, concerts, and credit card offers.

Frustrated, Matt went home.

He'd tried to call Shana several times, but only got a busy signal. Things were not looking good.

Matt found his mother in the kitchen. The twins were asleep in their crib, set in the doorway between the kitchen and dining room.

"Hey, Mom. Shana didn't call, did she?"

Mrs. Camden shook her head. "I don't think so."

Matt dropped into a chair and ran his hands through his thick hair. His broad shoulders slouched.

My son, the picture of romantic despair, Mrs. Camden thought.

"What's wrong?" she asked him finally.

"Shana and I had kind of a really stupid fight last night. So I'm just going to apologize."

"Apologizing is good," Mrs. Camden replied noncommittally.

"Even if it's not your fault?"

Mrs. Camden smiled. "So what are you going to say?" she asked.

"That I'm sorry for sounding so self-righteous, because I was definitely wrong to take you out to the movies when you wanted to study."

Mrs. Camden nodded. "Sounds good so far."

"And I'll also say I was wrong to take advantage of you just because you have an apartment and I don't."

Mrs. Camden raised her eyebrows.

"We use her apartment to *study*, Mom," Matt insisted.

"I get it," Mrs. Camden said, looking toward heaven.

"And then I guess I'll say that I just didn't understand what you were getting at, but I do now…"

Mrs. Camden nodded again.

"Although if you wanted to tell me something, you could try just telling me it, not sending out secret female signals no guy could possibly understand!"

"I don't think you want to go down *that* route," Mrs. Camden said.

"How about if I just say, 'You were right, Shana,'" Matt continued. "And that your always being right is what I like most about you. Not to mention that you're so cute and wonderful and sexy."

"Hmm?" Mrs. Camden replied.

"It works, right?" Matt asked.

"Except for that 'cute and wonderful and sexy' part."

"What's wrong with it?"

"Shana's a smart girl," Mrs. Camden said. "She'll think you're being patronizing to her."

"*Being patronizing!*" Matt cried. "I was pouring my heart out!"

"Keep working on it," Mrs. Camden suggested.

While she made a salad, Matt dialed Shana's number from the kitchen phone. The line was still busy.

Who can she be talking to? Matt asked himself. *Is she telling all her friends what a jerk I am?*

Mrs. Camden glanced at the clock. "Where could your father be?"

"Is something the matter?" Matt asked.

Mrs. Camden wiped her hands. "Your father said he was going to take a half day down at the church.

"Well, that was five hours ago, and there are things to do here, things I really need him for."

"He'll be home, Mom," Matt said. "He probably had an emergency or something."

"I just hope—" But Mrs. Camden stopped herself before she said too much.

"You just hope what?" Matt asked.

"Never mind," Mrs. Camden replied.

It's too soon for Matt to know what's going on, she decided. *And I almost spilled the beans.*

"I guess I'll call the housing office again," Matt said. "May I use the phone in your bedroom? I want to keep the other line open in case Shana calls."

"Why are you calling the housing office?"

Just then, Rev. Camden came through the back door.

"Hi, Dad. Bye, Dad," Matt said. He was gone before Mrs. Camden could stop him.

"Your son is planning to move out," Mrs. Camden announced in an angry tone. She turned her back on her husband and began to chop carrots.

Rev. Camden checked his watch and frowned. *I knew I was late,* he thought. *Just not* this *late*.

He walked over to his wife and wrapped his arms around her waist.

"I'm sorry, honey," he whispered, giving her a peck on the cheek. "The Moons dropped in for an unscheduled counseling session."

"The Moons?" Mrs. Camden said, surprised. "As in Jimmy Moon?"

Rev. Camden nodded.

"I didn't even know they went to our church."

"They don't."

Silence hung in the air for a moment. Then Mrs. Camden looked hard at her husband.

"You know I can't talk about it!" he cried. "It's confidential."

Mrs. Camden continued to chop carrots.

"But I *can* talk about the fact that the deacons are up to something," Rev. Camden continued.

Mrs. Camden rolled her eyes.

"No, seriously, they are!" Rev. Camden insisted. "Lou walked into my office today, and he obviously didn't expect to see me there. He looked as if I'd caught him with his hand in the cookie jar."

Mrs. Camden chopped the carrots furiously.

"And yesterday," her husband went on, "one of the other deacons—" He stopped when Mrs. Camden pushed past him and went over to the stove.

"You don't want to hear any more, do you?" Rev. Camden asked sheepishly.

"No," Mrs. Camden said as she pulled a pan of macaroni and cheese out of the oven and placed it on a wooden tray.

"Okay," Rev. Camden sighed. "I know I'm late. Tell me what I can do to get back into your good graces."

Mrs. Camden handed him a pile of plates, a bunch of napkins, and a bundle of silverware.

"Set the table?" Rev. Camden said in disbelief.

"For starters," Mrs. Camden replied.

"I'll get right on it."

On his way upstairs, Matt found his little brother in the foyer. Simon held his catcher's mitt in one hand and a bottle of cooking oil in the other.

"Hey, Matt!" Simon chirped.

"What's with the cooking oil?"

Simon shrugged. "Oil is oil, right?"

"You're supposed to use neat's-foot oil," his brother informed him.

"There wasn't any," Simon said defensively.

"You didn't oil your glove with Wesson, did you?" Matt said.

Simon looked guilty. "Did I say I oiled my glove with this?"

Matt shook his head. "Leave that glove in the hot sun and it'll start smelling like a hamburger."

"So?" Simon replied. "I like hamburgers." Then he whipped a baseball from his jacket pocket. "Think quick!" he cried.

The ball flew at Matt, who snatched it out of the air effortlessly.

Simon was impressed. "How about throwing for a while?" he asked.

"Sorry," Matt replied. "I have to call Shana—"

Suddenly, he tossed the baseball back to Simon. "Think quick!" he cried.

Simon missed the catch. The baseball sailed across the foyer. As Simon and Matt watched in horror, the ball crashed through a tiny window beside the front door.

Simon turned on his brother. "You've got to warn me!"

Matt shrugged. "I said, 'Think quick.'"

"'Think quick' could mean *anything!*" Simon cried. "What kind of warning is that?"

Mrs. Camden rushed into the room.

"I heard breaking glass!" she said. "What did you two destroy now?"

Matt and Simon exchanged guilty glances. Mrs. Camden spotted the window.

"Oh, no!" she moaned. "What did I tell you about baseball in the house?"

"It will never happen again," Simon promised.

"Pray he never takes up bowling," Matt quipped, and bolted upstairs.

"Who was that rushing by?" Mary asked as she tied the laces of her sneakers.

Lucy looked up from her book. "Just Matt," she replied. "He's probably using Mom's phone to call Shana again."

"Poor sap," Mary said, shaking her head. "I think she dumped him."

"Where are *you* going?" Lucy asked.

"To throw some balls with Simon. He's going out for the baseball team, and try-outs start tomorrow."

Lucy nodded, not really listening. Mary felt Lucy's eyes on her.

"What?" Mary demanded.

Lucy shrugged. "Nothing."

"Something's up," Mary said. "I know it. You've been staring off into space for the last half hour."

"You're right," Lucy sighed.

Mary flipped on the desk lamp and shone the light into Lucy's face.

"You vill tell ze truth or suffer ze consequences!" Mary said in a lame imitation of a movie villain.

Lucy actually laughed.

It occurred to Mary that it was the first time her sister had smiled in the last twenty-four hours.

Something really is *bothering her,* Mary decided. She suddenly felt protective of Lucy.

"Have you seen Jimmy Moon lately?" Lucy asked, her voice a whisper.

"He's not on my VIP list," Mary said, trying to keep things light. "Why?"

"Well," Lucy began, hesitant to voice her fears, "I haven't really talked to Jimmy all year. Because of the breakup."

"You mean because he *dumped* you," Mary corrected.

"He didn't dump me!" Lucy cried. Mary gave her a look that said, *Get real.*

"Okay," Lucy relented. "He *did* dump me. The *first* time. The second time, *I* dumped *him.* And I know I hurt his feelings."

Mary rolled her eyes.

"Anyway," Lucy stumbled on, "I...I saw him coming out of the school counselor's office today."

"No big deal," Mary said. "I was there yesterday, to give them a note from the doctor about my pulled ligament."

Lucy looked away. "It's not like that. You should have seen his face, Mary."

"His face?"

"Something is wrong with him," Lucy said. "A bad something."

"A *bad* something? Isn't that a little dramatic?" Mary said.

"He doesn't look right," Lucy insisted. "He's acting paranoid."

Mary felt her sister's alarm. "Drugs?" she whispered.

Lucy shrugged. "Maybe," she replied. "Or maybe he's just choosing bad friends."

"Like who?" Mary demanded.

Lucy sighed. "Like...those guys who hang out behind the football field."

Mary grabbed Lucy. "I want you to listen to me."

Lucy pulled away. "I'm listening," she said, frowning.

"If Jimmy Moon looks like he's doing drugs, and he's hanging out with guys who look like they *sell* drugs…then maybe you should just stay away from him."

"You're right," Lucy sighed. "Unless…"

Mary whirled around. "Unless what?"

"Unless I'm the one who caused it."

Mary stared at her sister. "Excuse me?"

"I may be the one responsible," Lucy said.

"*You* caused Jimmy Moon to take drugs?"

"Maybe," Lucy replied. "He never hooked up with anyone after me. Maybe he's sad and lonely. Maybe he never got over me."

Mary tapped her foot. "So he turned to a life of drugs?"

"Is that so hard to believe?" Lucy cried defensively.

"How do you know Ashley didn't lead him astray?" Mary said.

"Please," Lucy said, shaking her head. "You know it was me. Ashley is *Vogue* on the outside and vague on the inside."

"I agree with you about Ashley," Mary conceded. "But I still don't think it was you who wrecked Jimmy Moon's life."

"Why not?"

"We don't even know for sure that Jimmy is doing drugs."

Lucy nodded.

"But," Mary said, "if he *is*, I am really certain that it has absolutely nothing—repeat!—*nothing* to do with *you!*"

Lucy didn't seem convinced.

"Okay." Mary tried again. "I want you to listen to me. This is your big sister talking."

Lucy sighed, prepared for a lecture.

"You want to jump in and save this guy, but drugs are serious business. Just stay away from Jimmy Moon."

Lucy said nothing. Mary faced the mirror and adjusted her baseball cap.

"Can I ask you another favor?" Lucy said.

"What?"

"Go play ball with Simon," Lucy replied. "I can't concentrate when you're around."

Ruthie had seen so much of Matt's telephone action in the last few days that she decided it might make a pretty good game to play. She set up the table in her room for an elaborate tea-and-telephone party.

First she retrieved her little teapot and matching cups from her toy box.

After she set the table, Ruthie gathered

some of her favorite dolls and stuffed animals and placed them in tiny chairs around the table.

Next Ruthie dragged out her toy phone—the one with the battery-operated bell that rang when you pressed the button.

But when she tested it, she discovered that the batteries were dead.

Ruthie ran into her mom's bedroom and snatched the cordless telephone from the dresser.

"I've got my friends, and I've got a phone," Ruthie said. "Let the party begin!"

Matt looked into his parents' room. He was disappointed to discover that the cradle for the cordless telephone was empty.

Mom must have left the phone downstairs, Matt thought.

He couldn't go back downstairs and face his mother again. He didn't want to talk to her about moving out—his embarrassment about the broken window outweighed his need for privacy.

Matt went over to the bedstand and picked up the main phone. He carried it to the door, but the cord was too short to reach even the hallway.

Matt took a deep breath, lifted the

receiver, and dialed. Three rings later, an answering machine picked up.

"Hi!" the machine said in a melodious voice. "This is Shana. Sorry I'm not in to take your call. How about leaving me a message?"

Matt waited for the beep. But before he could get a word out, the phone line clicked and he heard a dial tone.

There must be something wrong with the machine, Matt decided.

He pressed "redial."

Ruthie was holding the cordless phone when it rang.

"Our first caller," she informed her teddy bear.

She pressed the "on" button. "Hello?" she said into the receiver.

"Hi," a perky young woman replied. "This is Shana. Who am I talking to?"

"It's Ruthie," the little girl answered.

"Hi, Ruthie," said Shana. "Is Matt around?"

Ruthie scanned her room. Then she peeked through the door out into the empty hallway.

"No," Ruthie said politely. "Matt isn't around."

"Oh," Shana said, sounding disappointed. "Could you give him a message for me, please? I'm calling from a pay phone and he can't reach me."

Ruthie fidgeted in her chair. Her telephone game wasn't so much fun anymore.

"Tell Matt that my answering machine isn't working. I have the kind of machine with the phone attached, and the phone isn't working, either…"

"Uh-huh," Ruthie said, paying absolutely no attention.

"So even if he wanted to talk to me, he won't be able to…"

Ruthie put down the phone and lifted her cup. She took a long sip of air. Then she put the phone to her ear again. She was annoyed to hear Matt's girlfriend still droning on about something or other.

"I just wanted him to know I'm really sorry, that's all," Shana concluded.

"Am I supposed to be writing all this down?" Ruthie asked, after a long pause.

"Too much to remember, huh?" Shana asked.

Ruthie nodded. "For an eight-year-old," she replied.

"I'm sorry," Shana said. "Just…just tell your brother that I called, okay?"

"Okay," Ruthie said, twirling a lock of her hair.

Just then, Ruthie heard Simon call her name. She turned off the phone and ran into the hall.

Simon was waiting for her at the top of the stairs.

"There you are!" he cried. "Just the person I wanted to see!"

Ruthie was incredulous. "Me?" she said. "Are you okay, Simon?"

"I admit, I'm a little desperate," he confessed. "Mary's stalling me. She's having some kind of important discussion with Lucy, and she can't help me just now."

"What do you want *me* for?" Ruthie asked suspiciously.

"How about if we go to the backyard and throw the ball around a little?"

Ruthie held out her hands. Simon tossed the ball gently. Ruthie caught it with both hands and examined it closely. She even squeezed it a few times.

"It isn't a piece of fruit!" Simon said, disgusted.

"Why do you want to play baseball?" Ruthie seemed genuinely curious.

Simon crossed his arms. "Because baseball is a game of skill and grace," he explained. "And it's the only sport that really tests my razor-sharp reflexes, okay?"

"What's for dinner?" Ruthie asked suddenly.

"Why?" Simon asked.

Ruthie sniffed the air. "'Cause I smell hamburger." She looked at Simon's glove. He quickly tore it from his hand and thrust the mitt behind his back.

"Why does that thing smell like hamburger?"

"It doesn't smell like hamburger," Simon insisted.

"Hamburger," Ruthie said, nodding. "*And* onions."

Simon thrust out his hand. "Just give me the ball, Ruthie."

"I'll play catch with you. I love the smell of hamburger." Ruthie tossed the ball back to Simon. Even though he was only a few steps away, he fumbled the catch. The ball bopped him on the head and bounced down the steps. Before the ball finally came to rest, it ricocheted off the front door with a loud bang.

"Ow!" Simon yelped. "I wasn't ready!"

Ruthie laughed. "Maybe you should get your razor sharpened."

Mary appeared just then. "Looks like

you need a lot of work," she said.

Simon smiled. "Are you going to throw now?"

Mary nodded. "I'm all yours for the next two hours."

"Great!" Simon cried.

"Too bad," Ruthie sighed. "I think baseball with a hamburger smell would have been fun."

With a toss of her head, she returned to her tea party.

Matt pressed the "redial" button. Again, Shana's machine answered, then hung up on him before he could leave a message.

He wanted to scream in frustration. But he regained his control and hung up. Out in the hallway, he spotted Ruthie heading for her room.

"Hey, Ruthie," Matt greeted her.

"Hello," his little sister replied. "Do you want to join my tea party?"

"I can't," Matt answered. "I have to go back to school and check the bulletin boards."

"What for?"

"I'm looking for a place to live."

"You have a place to live!"

Matt smiled. "I mean a place closer to

the school. So I won't have to travel so far every day."

"Why do you want to live somewhere else?" Ruthie asked.

Matt knelt down and faced his little sister. "Sometimes a big person like me needs privacy," he explained.

"So you can kiss your girlfriend!" Ruthie said, nodding.

Matt laughed. Then he turned serious.

"Ruthie, I might be getting a call from Shana while I'm gone."

Ruthie nodded.

"Will you tell me if she calls?" Matt asked.

"Okay," Ruthie said softly.

"It's a very important phone call," Matt continued.

"How come?" Ruthie demanded.

"Not 'How come,'" Matt corrected her. "*Why.*"

Ruthie grew exasperated. "That's what I asked you!"

"No," Matt corrected her again. "'Why' is it important?"

"That's what I'm asking!" Ruthie's voice rose to a wail.

Matt stood up and shook his head. "Why am I trying to teach grammar?" he muttered.

Ruthie shrugged. "I don't know."

"Look," Matt said finally. "This call is important because I really like this girl and I'd like to spend more time with her."

Ruthie nodded. "Is that why you're moving out?"

"I'm not moving out yet," Matt told her. "And that's not the point, anyway."

"But I don't want you to move away," Ruthie said. "I'll never see you again."

Matt smiled. "I'll just be a short drive away," he insisted.

Ruthie shrugged. "Whatever. But if you're moving out because of Shana, I don't think I like her."

Matt sighed. "Just tell me if Shana calls while I'm out," he said.

Matt left, and Ruthie returned to her room.

"Well!" she told her party guests. "He said to tell him if she calls later. He didn't ask me if she called already."

Then Ruthie smiled.

All she had to do was keep Matt and Shana apart and Matt would never leave! And if Matt never left, Ruthie would have her older brother all to herself, forever.

THREE

Matt parked near the campus green and headed for the student center. He paused at one of the outdoor bulletin boards.

There were no notices about vacant apartments. But there were lots of "apartment wanted" signs.

Suddenly two hands covered his eyes. Soft, cool, perfumed hands. A woman's hands.

"Guess who?" a young woman teased.

The voice was familiar, but Matt couldn't place it.

"I don't know," he replied. "But I'd like to take my time guessing."

Matt whirled around.

"Connie!" he cried, hugging the owner of the hands.

The pretty young woman who had been Matt's high school prom date smiled up at him. She had cut her dark hair even shorter, but her smile was as bright as ever.

"Surprised?" Connie laughed.

"You bet!"

"I haven't seen you since graduation," Connie said.

"I haven't been around much, either."

"It's really great to see you," Connie said. "I don't know many people here. Just my roommates."

"I didn't even know you were going to college," Matt said.

"I'm not. Not technically. Not yet."

Matt cocked his head.

"Well, as you know, I wasn't the best student in high school," Connie said regretfully. "So I'm going to audit some courses this spring. And if I do okay, I'll officially enroll in September."

"That's great," Matt said. "I'm sure you'll do fine."

"Thanks." Connie pointed at the bulletin board. "What are you looking for?"

Matt shrugged. "A room. An apartment to share, a big cardboard box—anything to get out of my parents' house."

"You've got that right!" Connie laughed.

"Since the twins were born, living at home has been a little harder than I anticipated," Matt explained.

"Really?" Connie said. "Well, I might just have a solution."

"I need all the help I can get," Matt said.

"My two girlfriends and I are looking for a fourth person to share our two-bedroom apartment," Connie said.

How would Shana feel about me living with three women? Matt wondered.

"Are you sure that would work?" he asked.

Connie nodded. "Why not? We're all nice girls. I think you'd like us."

"I don't know," Matt said slowly.

"Come on, Matt!" Connie urged. "I'm sure you'd like Charlotte and Amanda. They're cool and easy to get along with. We're friends, right? Give it a try."

Connie tore off a corner of one of the posters on the bulletin board and pulled a pen from her purse. Before Matt could object, she scribbled her phone number and address on the paper.

"You really think this would be okay?" Matt asked, still unconvinced.

"Sure!" Connie laughed. "It'd be fun

having a guy around."

She thrust the paper into Matt's hands. "Come over later tonight. Everyone will be there and you can meet us all."

"All right," Matt said, nodding. "I'll be there."

Connie checked her watch. "Yikes! I've got to go."

Matt studied the address on the paper. The location was perfect, and living with three women definitely sounded interesting.

He tucked the paper into his pocket and headed back to his car.

At home, Rev. Camden was worried.

He was supposed to be finishing his sermon for Sunday. It would be his first church service since coming back from paternity leave, and he wanted it to be special. But he was torn by doubt.

Just what was Lou doing in my office this morning? he wondered. *And why is everyone at the church avoiding me?*

Rev. Camden knew that something was going on behind his back, and he didn't like it.

Clutching a pad in one hand and a pencil in the other, Rev. Camden went up to his bedroom. His wife was there, changing the twins.

"You look tired," Mrs. Camden said.

"This Sunday's sermon is just not coming to me," he confessed.

"It's only Tuesday."

"You know," Rev. Camden said, "maybe I should go down to the church to work for an hour or so."

Mrs. Camden frowned. "Why don't you stick around?"

Just then, Matt appeared.

"I'm back!" he announced. "Did Shana call?"

"Sorry, Matt," Mrs. Camden said.

"I thought she might have called on your private line, that's all," Matt replied.

"How could she know the number?" Mrs. Camden asked.

"You know," Matt said, "I'm an adult. You could just give me the number."

Rev. Camden smiled. "We could. But why exactly would we do that?"

"Because the kids keep the other line tied up," Matt replied. "So people—namely Shana—couldn't get through even if they—she—wanted to."

"Okay," Mrs. Camden told him. "You have my permission to tell whoever's tying up the line right now to please get off so that their brother can make a very important phone call."

Matt frowned. "Thanks. Thanks a lot."

"That's what we're here for," Rev. Camden joked.

But Matt was not amused. "Connie was right," he muttered.

"Connie?" Rev. Camden jumped in. "I thought we were talking about Shana."

Mrs. Camden thrust one of the twins into Rev. Camden's arms as Matt headed off to make his call.

"Here," she said. "This one won't need to make a phone call for years."

"I hate to say this, but…" Rev. Camden's voice trailed off.

"But?" Mrs. Camden prompted.

"You remember when I was trying to find an apartment for Shana?"

Mrs. Camden nodded.

"I gave her both telephone numbers. Maybe she doesn't want to talk to Matt."

"Then she'd be crazy," Mrs. Camden said. "Trust me, Shana will call."

Rev. Camden sighed. "If only a simple phone call would solve *my* problem."

Mrs. Camden touched her husband's shoulder. "You've been a hardworking minister for twenty years. If this sermon doesn't knock them off their feet, they'll find it in their hearts to forgive you."

"Yeah," Rev. Camden said. "Everybody loves me. That may not keep me from being fired, though."

Mrs. Camden's eyes widened. "Fired!" she cried. "What are you talking about?"

"I didn't want to worry you," Rev. Camden said in a low voice.

"Why would you be fired?" Mrs. Camden demanded.

"It's just a feeling I'm getting. I thought it was because I was away so long. But the way Lou breezed into my office today..."

Mrs. Camden patted her husband's shoulder again. "He didn't know you were there," she said.

But her husband looked miserable.

"Come on," Mrs. Camden said. "The deacons know how valuable you are. They understand that you are busy right now."

"Maybe they think I'm a little *too* busy," Rev. Camden shot back. "Maybe they think I can't handle the job."

Mrs. Camden kissed his cheek. "Could you please just stick around for the rest of the evening?" she pleaded. "Give me tonight to get organized. Then tomorrow you can spend as much time as you need at the church."

Rev. Camden put his free arm around his wife. "All right," he said.

Just then, the telephone rang in the living room. Rev. and Mrs. Camden listened as Matt ran downstairs to answer it. He returned a minute later, cordless in hand.

"It's for you," he said, offering the phone to his father.

"Thanks, son."

"You know I'm expecting a call," Matt added.

"I'll try to keep it brief."

Matt looked at the phone on the nightstand. "Maybe you could call Lou back on *your* line," he suggested.

Mrs. Camden pointed to the door. "Out," she commanded.

"Hello, Lou," Rev. Camden said into the phone. "What a coincidence. I was just working on this Sunday's sermon..."

"So how did I do?" Simon asked.

Mary tugged off her glove and baseball cap, trying to think of an answer that wouldn't dash Simon's hopes.

"Pretty good," she said finally. "You've got the signals down. And you've learned some cool moves from watching the pros on television. But you still need to work on actually catching the ball."

Simon shrugged. "I know," he admitted. "But tryouts are tomorrow. This is all the practice I could get in before then."

"Why didn't you start sooner?" Mary asked.

"It was a last-minute decision," Simon explained. "I wasn't sure I wanted to go out for the team until the other day."

"Why?" Mary was curious.

Simon hesitated. "It's expected."

Mary was surprised. "*Expected?*"

"Sure," Simon replied. "You're an athlete. Matt's pretty good. As the next male Camden, I should carry on the tradition."

"You don't have to do something just because people expect it," Mary explained.

"Boy," Simon said. "Are you naive."

"Me? Naive?" Mary said.

"Sure," Simon said. "You know that deep down in their hearts, Mom and Dad want us to succeed."

"Well, duh," Mary said.

"Athletics—in my case, baseball—is a road to that success."

"Listen, Simon," Mary said patiently. "Mom and Dad love us and they want us to be successful. But I don't think they care if we play sports or not."

Simon looked at Mary doubtfully. "That's easy for the best girls' basketball player at school to say," he told her. "But I have to create my own legacy."

Rev. Camden didn't like the direction his conversation with Lou was going.

"We know how busy you are," Lou was saying. "So we thought we'd give you a break."

Rev. Camden raised one eyebrow at his wife. Mrs. Camden put her ear to the phone so she could listen, too.

"But I just had a break," Rev. Camden said.

"We think we can help you even more," Lou replied. "We thought we could put out the church bulletin ourselves."

Rev. Camden's jaw dropped. "But I always do the bulletin!"

"I know," Lou said. "But you're a brand-new father. Sid and I will take care of it. All we need is the title of your sermon."

"The title of my sermon," Rev. Camden repeated. He looked at his wife helplessly. She shrugged.

"It's, uh…" Rev. Camden thought for a

moment. Then an idea hit him.

"The name of the sermon is 'Twenty Years of My Life,'" he said finally.

"Terrific!" Lou said. "Thanks, Reverend Camden. Sorry to have bothered you."

"No problem," Rev. Camden lied. "Good night, Lou."

He hung up. "I'm sure of it now," Rev. Camden said. "There's something going on."

Later, Rev. and Mrs. Camden were in the kitchen, making dinner.

Matt walked in, smiling.

"I won't be here for eats," he announced.

"Shana?" Mrs. Camden asked.

"Connie," Matt replied.

His parents did a double take.

"It's not what you think," Matt explained. "I just got lucky with my housing search."

"Housing search?" Mrs. Camden said.

"Wait a minute," Rev. Camden interrupted. "Who is Connie?"

"You remember Connie, Dad," Matt replied. "From church. The girl I took—"

"To the prom!" Rev. Camden cried, slapping his forehead. "Right."

"She and two other girls want me to move in with them."

"Move *in?*" Mrs. Camden cried. "You and three *women?* My innocent little boy and three worldly women?"

"It's not definite yet," Matt said. He could see his parents were uncomfortable with the idea. "I know what you're both thinking," he added. "But it's not like when you were in school. Nowadays it's very common for men and women to share housing."

Rev. Camden and Mrs. Camden nodded, clearly not buying that argument.

"We're more mature at our age than you were," Matt tried to tell them.

His parents nodded again.

"Connie and I are just friends," Matt insisted. "Besides, her apartment is within walking distance of school. If the rent is split four ways, it's cheaper than a dorm room—and probably quieter, too."

"Hey," Mrs. Camden said, throwing up her hands. "It's your life and your money."

She left the kitchen, clearly upset.

Rev. Camden looked at his son.

"You know that she can have your room painted like a nursery in twenty-four hours," he said.

"Meaning what?" Matt asked.

"Meaning that you'd better be sure you know what you're doing, son."

Matt nodded.

"And by the way," Rev. Camden added, "you *don't* know what you're doing."

Connie was preparing her two roommates for their first meeting with Matt.

"He's really cool," Connie began. "He's laid-back. Quiet. The perfect roommate."

"Is he nice?" asked Charlotte, a tall girl with freckles and long red hair.

Connie nodded. "Very. He's the oldest son in a big family, so he knows how to share. And he's the son of a minister, so he's very responsible."

"Yuck!" Amanda, a blonde with big blue eyes, cried in alarm. "You didn't say anything about *that!*"

"Hey!" Connie protested. "Would I have gone to my one and only prom with a loser?" She glanced at her watch. "Matt'll be here any minute now," she said. "I hope he can find a place to park."

"He has his own car," Charlotte said, nodding. "That's a plus."

"But is he *really* quiet?" Amanda asked. "You know how guys always want to crank their stereos up real loud."

Connie shook her head. "That's not Matt. He's clean, quiet, and considerate."

"What about when guys come?" Charlotte said. "Isn't he going to get in the way?"

"And we're not going to be able to walk around the apartment in our underwear with a guy here," Amanda added.

"I'm more worried about him walking around in *his* underwear!" Charlotte said.

Connie smiled. "You haven't seen Matt yet."

Amanda made a face. Just then, there was a knock at the door.

Connie straightened her clothes and opened the door.

"Hey, Matt!" she greeted him. "Come on in."

When Charlotte and Amanda saw Matt, all their objections were forgotten.

"Hi," Matt said shyly.

"Hello," Charlotte breathed.

"Hey," Amanda whispered in awe.

The four of them stood around looking at one another for a moment.

"So," Charlotte said finally. "When can you move in?"

Connie laughed and took Matt's arm. "I

think maybe you guys should introduce yourselves first.

As Matt shook the girls' hands, he found himself more than a little impressed. Amanda was cute, with a ready smile. Charlotte seemed very sweet, and she was very pretty, too. For the first time in the last twenty-four hours, all thoughts of Shana were driven from Matt's mind.

"It's nice to meet you," he said with a sincere smile. "Both of you."

"Why don't I show you what would be your bedroom?" Connie said. "The three of us would take the bigger one," she explained.

Matt followed Connie into the back bedroom. When he was out of sight, Charlotte and Amanda exchanged looks.

"Whoa!" Amanda cried, fanning herself.

"Nice," Charlotte agreed. "Very nice."

"Gorgeous," Amanda went on. "Did you see those shoulders?"

Charlotte nodded. "I'll give it a go," she whispered.

"I'm game," Amanda said.

Just then, Connie and Matt returned.

"This is the living room," Connie said. "The kitchenette you can see over there."

"And we have a balcony, too!" Charlotte added enthusiastically.

"So what do you think?" Amanda asked.

Matt shrugged. "It looks great!"

The three women exchanged glances.

"Okay," Connie said. "If we're going to do this, we should have some rules."

"Sure." Matt nodded.

"Of course," Charlotte agreed. "Rules."

"Absolutely," Amanda added.

"Like what?" Charlotte asked.

"Well, let's see," Connie said slowly. "Like, no one dates anyone else in the apartment."

"That's right," Amanda added. "That wouldn't work at all. What else?"

"No sleepover guests," Charlotte suggested.

Everyone nodded in agreement.

"And no parties," Connie said. "Unless we all agree to have one."

Matt listened attentively as Connie and the others outlined the domestic details of the arrangement. The four of them talked for a long time.

"So," Connie said. "There is no reason this shouldn't work out, right?"

*   *   *

Mrs. Camden was finishing up the dishes when Matt returned with company.

"Hello, Mrs. Camden."

"Why, hello, Connie," Matt's mother greeted her with an affectionate peck. "How are you? How is your father?"

"I'm fine, thanks," Connie replied. "And so is Pop. He just retired, did you know?"

"No, I didn't," Mrs. Camden said. "Tell him congratulations."

"And congratulations on your twins, too," Connie returned.

"So," Mrs. Camden said casually, "what are you two up to?"

"I just came by to get some stuff and check my messages," Matt replied.

"No messages," Mrs. Camden said. "What kind of stuff?"

Matt smiled. "The girls thought it would be fun if all of us were there together tonight."

"We also thought we'd feel safer with Matt around," Connie added. "It's only our first week in the place."

"Why don't you both help yourselves to some of the leftover ham?" Mrs. Camden suggested. "I'll go upstairs and get some stuff together for you."

While they were making sandwiches,

Connie stood next to Matt. As he piled meat and cheese onto a bun, Connie leaned over and kissed him.

Matt was surprised and flattered. "That was nice," he said. "But what about the rules?"

Connie blushed. "Oh, that's right. The rules. Sorry."

"It's okay," Matt replied. "We're not dating. Nobody's dating. Right?"

Connie grinned. "Right."

Matt decided to tell Connie about Shana. But before he could, they were interrupted by Mrs. Camden's return.

"That's all you'll be needing for tonight," she said, handing him a duffel bag. "You can come by and pick up more tomorrow."

"Thanks, Mom," Matt said.

After they finished their sandwiches, Matt and Connie got ready to leave. Rev. Camden came in from his study.

"Annie tells me you're going to give apartment life a try," he said to Matt when Connie stepped away for a minute.

"It will be a growing experience," Matt said.

"You and three women," Rev. Camden said, shaking his head. "It certainly will be."

FOUR

Matt tossed and turned in the unfamiliar bed. Finally, he rolled over and lifted his watch from the nightstand. It was almost one in the morning.

His first evening in the apartment had been fun. He and the three girls had ordered food and watched a comedy on cable. Amanda could do a pretty good impression of Madonna, and she entertained them all, karaoke-style.

At midnight, Connie said good night. Amanda and Charlotte soon joined her in their huge bedroom, and Matt headed for his own, much smaller room.

In the dark, Matt thought about Shana.

He would have stopped by her place earlier, but Connie was with him, and that would have been awkward. He had never gotten a chance to call Shana again, and now it was too late.

While Matt liked Shana a lot, he had to admit there were problems between them. And he was surprised at how much fun he'd been having with his new roommates. It was exciting to meet new girls.

But Shana was special. Connie was nice, but beyond their night at the prom, they hadn't spoken much. And he hardly knew Charlotte and Amanda.

But they were both *very* attractive.

If you really like one girl, then what does it mean when you're attracted to another girl? Or three girls? he wondered.

Matt couldn't decide. And all this thinking was making him restless.

He snapped on the desk lamp and fumbled through his book bag until he found his laboratory manual. He figured he might as well use his insomnia to study extra hard for his quiz tomorrow.

But Matt's interest in chemistry waned quickly. He dropped the lab manual on the nightstand. *I'm starving,* he decided.

Remembering the leftovers in the refrigerator, he rose and threw on a pair of gym shorts, then peeked out the door.

The girls' door was closed. Matt tiptoed quietly down the hall.

He was reaching into the refrigerator for the remains of his Dairy Shack sub when he felt soft hands on his back. Matt spun around.

Charlotte was standing there, wearing a big smile on her face. She was hardly wearing anything else—just a tiny light blue teddy-bear nightie.

Matt swallowed hard.

"Can I help?" Charlotte asked.

"I was just—" Before Matt could finish his sentence, Charlotte placed her soft mouth over his.

Matt's eyes went wide as Charlotte's lips grew more insistent. For a moment, he resisted. But only for a moment.

As they kissed, Amanda walked into the kitchen and froze. She stepped back into the shadows before she was seen.

Then she went back to the bedroom.

Okay, Amanda thought. *You've made the first move, Charlotte.*

But tomorrow is my *turn.*

"Can Dianne wear that skirt any shorter?" Mary asked, eyeing her fellow classmate.

"It seems to work," Lucy observed.

"She's surrounded by guys."

"Yeah." Mary sighed wistfully.

"But would you go out with one of *those* guys?" Lucy added. Then she stopped.

Mary followed her sister's gaze.

Lucy was watching one of several punks who hung out behind the football field.

"Come on!" Mary said, tapping Lucy. "We've got to go."

Lucy's eyes lingered on the guy for a moment. Then she followed her sister.

"Slow down!" she called. "I can't keep up with you."

Mary slowed until Lucy caught up.

"What's the hurry?" Lucy demanded.

Mary started counting off on her fingers. "First I've got to pick up Ruthie because Matt has moved out on us and left that job to me. Then I have to take you both home—"

"Then you're done!" Lucy interrupted.

Mary shook her head. "Not so!" she said sadly. "*Then* I've got to head over to the junior high so I can make Simon look good—which isn't going to be easy, the way he catches. And throws. And hits."

"You know he's using you," Lucy said.

Mary smiled. "He thinks that being

seen with me will help him make the team."

"So why are you doing it?" Lucy asked, waiting for Mary to unlock the car doors.

Mary shrugged. "It's kinda flattering, don't you think?" Then she paused.

Lucy turned around. The punk she'd seen earlier was crossing the lot, heading for a black sedan in a remote corner of the lot.

"Oh, no," Lucy gasped.

Jimmy Moon was sitting in the sedan, next to another kid. They were smoking something. As Lucy watched, they passed it back and forth, laughing.

"Let's go," Mary said.

But Lucy started walking straight toward the group.

The punk had swaggered up to the sedan and was leaning against it, talking to the kids inside. His thin lips curled into a sinister smile when he saw Lucy approach.

"Wait!" Mary cried. "Don't—"

"I'm just going to talk to him!" Lucy cried, her eyes fixed on Jimmy Moon.

"No, you're not!"

Lucy clutched her books to her chest. "I just want to find out what's going on."

Mary stamped her foot. "But he's not

your boyfriend anymore," she argued. "It's not your business!"

"Yes, it is—"

Lucy's words were interrupted by the sudden scream of police sirens.

With a squeal of tires on pavement, a Glenoak squad car raced through the parking lot toward the black sedan. Hordes of kids ran to the parking lot to get a better view. Lucy and Mary had the best seats in the house.

Lucy froze as the police car shot between her and the black sedan. The kid who had watched Lucy coming disappeared into the crowd.

The squad car skidded to a halt, and its doors flew open. Two uniformed policemen leapt out of the vehicle.

Their guns were drawn.

Someone in the crowd screamed.

Lucy took two steps backward, then turned and ran to Mary.

Jimmy Moon and the other kid threw up their hands and surrendered.

The cops ripped open the door and dragged Jimmy out of the seat. None too gently, they pushed Jimmy against the vehicle and searched him.

Lucy watched in shock as Jimmy Moon

was frisked—and the policeman drew a clear plastic bag from his pocket.

Jimmy turned around and saw the stash in the cop's hand.

Then he saw Lucy.

His eyes dropped as the policeman handcuffed him.

Then a school security guard appeared and dispersed the crowd.

Mary gathered her younger sister into her arms, but no words of comfort came to her lips, even as Lucy began to sob.

Rev. Camden sat in his church office, working on his computer. He tapped a few keys, then paused to squint at the flickering images on the screen. As he pored over the first draft of his Sunday sermon, he began to read it out loud.

"For twenty years of my life, this community has embraced me as its minister. And it is I who will"—Rev. Camden halted to correct a typo—"always remain in your debt. For you have given me untold joy, boundless satisfaction..."

Rev. Camden's voice trailed off. He shook his head.

What they've given me is excruciating paranoia, he thought bitterly. *The feeling of the noose as it gets tighter and tighter. You never know when the ax will fall.*

"Eric!" Lou cried.

The deacon was standing in his office, a stunned expression on his face.

"Lou?" Rev. Camden said.

"Wow!" the older man said. "You really scared me."

Rev. Camden smiled. "There I go again," he said. "Sitting at my own desk in my own office. Scaring people."

"Well, gosh, Eric," Lou stammered. "You're supposed to be at home."

Rev. Camden nodded. "Was there something you needed to get, Lou?"

Just then, a younger deacon, Sidney, arrived. "Yes!" Sid cried.

"Oh, yeah," Lou stammered. "We needed to get, ah…"

"Paper for the bulletin," Sid finished. "We want to get it printed right away."

"Well," Rev. Camden replied, "the copy shop on Maple does the printing. They donate the paper. I thought you knew that."

Lou nodded. So did Sid.

"All you have to do is supply the copy on disk," Rev. Camden continued. "Which, again, I am more than happy to do."

"We'll take care of it," Lou insisted. "You should be home with the new babies."

"You know," Rev. Camden said, "it's not too much for me to handle. I have a computer at home, and Mary can run the disk down to the copy shop."

"No!" Lou said. "We insist! We'll put the bulletin out this week."

Before Rev. Camden could protest, the doorbell buzzed.

"That's probably the mail," Lou said. "I'd better run and get it."

At almost the same time, Rev. Camden's phone rang. He answered it.

"Hey," a gruff voice said, "I'm looking for some guy named Lou. I think he's a deacon or something."

"I'm sorry," Rev. Camden said politely. "Lou just stepped out. I'll take a message."

"Look," the voice replied, "I just wanted to make sure that I had the right address... of the church."

Rev. Camden frowned. "What do you need our address for?"

"For the delivery," the man replied, "of the desk."

"Right," Rev. Camden said. "Well, can you tell me who ordered it?"

"Sure," the man answered readily. "Reverend Bergen. I guess he's the pastor or something."

Rev. Camden rubbed his forehead. His worst fears had been confirmed.

My congregation wants me out. They're going to fire me this week, probably after the Sunday service.

"Look, I'm sorry," Rev. Camden said finally. "There is no Reverend Bergen here." He hung up the phone. "Not yet, anyway," he muttered.

He got up and headed for Lou's office. But just as he stepped out his own door, Lucy ran inside. Her face was flushed, and she was completely out of breath.

"Dad!" she cried, and raced into his arms. "We—Mary and I—we saw your car, so Mary dropped me off—"

Lucy paused to catch her breath. Her cheeks were wet with tears.

"What's the matter, Lucy?" Rev. Camden said.

"It's Jimmy Moon," Lucy cried. "He just got busted—arrested—for marijuana possession. You've got to do something!"

"I was afraid of something like this," Rev. Camden said. "Sit down, Lucy."

"Why would I want to sit?" Lucy cried.

"Why aren't you springing into action? And what did you mean when you said you were afraid of something like this?"

"Nothing," Rev. Camden lied, giving Lucy a hug. "I just like to get all the facts before I spring into action, that's all."

"Since when?" she demanded. "Dad, this is important. Spring!"

Matt had managed to slip out of the apartment early that morning, before any of the girls were awake. His classes were a drag, and though he looked everywhere, he couldn't find Shana.

He tried calling her again, but the answering machine was still playing its old tricks.

Finally, between classes, Matt drove over to Shana's place. He sneaked past building security and took the elevator upstairs. Matt knocked on Shana's door.

There was no answer.

Matt decided to slip a note under the door. He went back to his car to get paper and a pen and wrote Shana a long, apologetic note. He was careful not to mention his new apartment. *She doesn't need to hear about it until I'm sure things are going to work out,* he rationalized.

But when he tried to go upstairs to deliver the note, Matt was nabbed by the security guard.

"Could you please give Shana this note?" Matt pleaded.

"What do I look like?" the guard said angrily. "A mailman?"

Defeated, Matt headed back to school.

When he arrived, he realized with horror that he'd left his lab manual on the nightstand in his new apartment.

He rushed back to the Camaro and drove quickly across town.

To his relief, no one was home. Matt hurried into his room and grabbed the book. He had just reached the front door when Amanda walked in.

"Hey, Matt," she greeted him. She had a strange look in her eyes.

"Uh...hi, Amanda," Matt said uncomfortably.

"Where are you going in such a hurry?"

"I've got a class," he answered.

But to Matt's surprise, Amanda blocked his way.

"So," she purred. "How did *you* sleep last night?"

"Fine." Matt shrugged, his mind racing. *She must be suspicious,* he thought.

"I saw you last night," she continued. "In the kitchen."

Matt froze in his tracks.

Busted!

"I don't know what you saw," Matt stammered. "But there is nothing going on between me and Charlotte."

Amanda smiled and leaned against Matt. Her big blue eyes looked into his.

"Well," she purred, "I want to be next in line for that same kind of nothing."

Matt nodded dumbly. "Gotta go!" he said, rushing out.

Connie arrived a moment later. "I just saw Matt running down the hall," she said. "What's going on?"

Amanda shrugged. "Nothing," she replied. "Not with *me*, anyway."

She looked hard at Connie. "We've got to talk about our new roomie," Amanda said.

"I'll do what I can. But I'm not sure what that should *be* yet," Rev. Camden said.

Lucy was shocked by her father's response. "Even I know what to do!"

Rev. Camden nodded. "Go on."

"There are parents to be called," Lucy said. "Programs to be recommended. Call

Sergeant Michaels, get down to the police station. Spring into action! Spring!"

Rev. Camden took his daughter's hand. "Why don't I drive you back to the house?" he suggested. "Then maybe I'll call Mr. and Mrs. Moon."

"That's not how you do it!" Lucy said. "If you've changed the way you operate, you should let a person know!"

"Let's take a deep breath, gather our thoughts, and think this through, all right?"

"*No!*" Lucy replied. "And why are you so calm? It's like you're not even worried— like you knew this was going to happen."

Then the realization dawned on her. "You *were* afraid, weren't you?" Lucy insisted. "Were you listening when I was talking to Mary yesterday?"

Rev. Camden shook his head. "That's not what happened," he said. "But I can't tell you how I knew, either. You have to trust me on this, Lucy." He went over to the computer and popped out the disk.

"We'll talk more about this later," he said. "Right now, I'm getting you home."

Rev. Camden shut down the computer and left the office. Lucy groaned in frustration and followed her father.

*   *   *

The baseball field was where Simon got in line to sign his name on the roster. He watched other kids throw, bat, and catch while the coach evaluated each performance.

Though he didn't know the person in front of him, Simon was feeling pretty nervous. Which meant that he was feeling pretty talkative, too.

"I'm going out for catcher," Simon announced, patting his mitt. "It's the best position, I think."

"Yeah," the other kid said absently. He was concentrating on the tryouts.

"Oh, yeah," Simon continued. "Everybody thinks that pitching is the best, but it's not. The catcher calls the pitches, makes great saves in the dirt, hustles down to first on every play, positions the outfield, fires the ball down to third after a strikeout... The catcher's position is awesome."

"Well, good luck," the kid said.

"We all need luck," Simon told him. "Only the best will be chosen to play."

"Don't get your hopes up," the kid said. "I hear that the coach's son is going out for catcher, too."

Simon suddenly felt sick. He hoped that his secret weapon would arrive soon.

"Simon!" Mary called from the sidelines. Simon spotted his sister and waved her over. As Mary crossed the field, he noticed the coach watching her. Simon slid up to the man's side.

"Hey, Coach," he said innocently, "I hope you don't mind if my sister watches for a while. She's really into sports. You may have heard of her. Mary Camden?"

The coach nodded. His eyes never left the field as another batter missed the first pitch.

"Mary Camden," Simon repeated. "Does that name ring a bell? Famous Reed basketball player, made varsity when she was a freshman?"

"Sure," the coach said. "I used to be her coach, way back when."

Simon beamed. "I guess being a jock runs in our family," he continued. "Must be in the genes or something."

"Great," the coach replied. "Look forward to seeing what you can do."

Then the coach sniffed the air. "Do I smell hamburger?"

Simon blushed. "Must be somebody barbecuing." He rushed off to meet Mary.

"Hey, Mary!" Simon cried. "Think quick!"

He shot the ball at her with his hardest and fastest throw. Mary snatched it out of the air with one gloveless hand.

"Hey, Simon!" she called back. "Sinking fastball."

Simon panicked, but gamely crouched to catch the ball.

The ball came fast. Simon scrambled to catch it, but it bounced off his glove and sailed past the coach. Kids on the sidelines laughed. A few parents laughed, too.

The coach retrieved the ball, then tossed it back to Simon.

Fortunately, he caught it *this* time. He smiled sheepishly at the coach.

This is the most embarrassing moment of my life, Simon thought.

All during the ride home, Rev. Camden stressed to Lucy that she wasn't to get involved with Jimmy Moon's problem. He tried to explain to her that the problem was between Jimmy and his parents.

"And the law," Lucy added.

"And the law," Rev. Camden agreed. "Which is all the more reason for you to stay out of it."

"Why?" Lucy asked.

"Because if Jimmy is in trouble with

drugs, then he is a dangerous person to be around," Rev. Camden told her.

"But I'm not stupid enough to be sucked into drugs," Lucy protested.

"I never said you were," Rev. Camden replied. "But that doesn't mean that being around Jimmy Moon couldn't hurt you in other ways."

"Like how?"

"If he is doing or dealing drugs, then he might get caught with lots of illegal stuff. And if you're with him, you might be arrested, too."

Lucy nodded.

"And," Rev. Camden continued, "if Jimmy was to owe his dealer some money, someone might come looking for him…"

"So?"

"So he might get hurt," Rev. Camden said. "And you might get hurt, too, just for being near him."

"You mean like a drive-by shooting or something?" Lucy's tone was incredulous.

"Or something." Rev. Camden nodded.

"Well, we don't have drive-by shootings in Glenoak," Lucy said. "And anyway, Jimmy is my friend."

"Which is why it's best for you not to get involved," Rev. Camden insisted. "Let

Jimmy work it out on his own, with the help of his parents."

Lucy didn't argue, but she was still unconvinced. As soon as they reached home, she grabbed the phone and dialed her friend Laura's number.

"Have you heard about Jimmy?" Lucy asked.

"Who hasn't?" Laura replied.

"Well, I was there when the police arrested them."

"Wow!" Laura cried. "But I thought you and Jimmy had broken up."

"We *did*," Lucy explained. "It was just a coincidence I was there, that's all."

They talked about the arrest for a few more minutes. Then Lucy got to the main reason for her call.

"Do you know the name of the other guy who was arrested?"

"No," Laura answered. "Why do you want to know?"

"No reason," Lucy lied. "I was just curious, that's all."

"Well, I don't know who that kid was," Laura said. "But I know the name of the one who got away!"

FIVE

Matt was starting to feel like a yo-yo. He'd run back and forth between school and Shana's for the last two days. He was neglecting his studies and burning enough gas to keep a refinery running.

But not today.

Today Matt planned to make a new start. Today he would act responsibly.

He had made it to his science class right on time. He'd finished his lab session and aced the quiz. He'd even made a stop at the library and grabbed the books he would need for next week's literature paper.

Matt checked his watch. He had an hour before his last class. He decided to try again to find Shana.

The security guard eyed Matt when he

entered Shana's building. Matt smiled, trying to assure him that he wouldn't attempt a break-in today.

Matt rang Shana's bell several times. She never answered it.

Frustrated, Matt ran back to the Camaro and rushed off to his next class.

As he raced away, Matt didn't notice Shana standing in the phone booth at the corner. She was dialing the Camden home again and again—and getting a busy signal.

It was Simon's turn. When his name was called, he stepped out onto the field, butterflies dancing in his stomach.

"Okay, Simon," the coach said. "I want to see your form and posture."

Simon got down into a squat and threw a few balls. He caught all the easy throws that came back at him without losing his balance.

The coach smiled. "Good form, Camden," he observed, writing something on the clipboard in his hand. "You've got the moves."

Simon grinned from ear to ear.

Next, the coach checked Simon's basic knowledge of signals. Simon passed that test with ease.

So far, so good, he thought.

"Let's try something else," the coach suggested.

He asked Simon to fire a few balls to each plate. Simon was good at hitting first and third, but most of Simon's longer throws, especially to second base, either fell short or went wild.

This is harder than it looks, Simon realized. He wiped the sweat out of his eyes.

Finally, the pitcher shot a few fastballs, low balls, and wide balls Simon's way. At first Simon was pretty good at catching them. But after a while he got tired.

A fastball smashed into his face mask. Simon saw stars. He stumbled and landed on his backside.

Simon's face grew hot when he heard laughter behind him. He got up and dusted off.

This time, he focused on the pitcher's windup.

The ball bounced out of Simon's mitt, ricocheted off the fence, and struck his helmet. This time it hurt his pride more than his body.

"Are you okay, son?" the coach called.

"Sure," Simon cried. He readjusted his helmet and crouched low. "Come on,

Coach," he insisted. "Let's do it."

The coach studied him for a moment. Then he signaled the pitcher to resume. More balls came Simon's way. He caught most—but not all—of them.

At least I stayed on my feet, Simon thought.

"Okay, Camden," the coach announced. "That's enough for today. Come back tomorrow for the next round."

Reluctantly, Simon headed for the dugout. Some of the kids snickered, but one boy, whom Simon didn't know, approached him.

"Hey," the kid said. "You were pretty good out there."

"Thanks," Simon replied, not sure whether the other boy was ribbing him.

"No, really," the kid continued. "Your posture's great, and you know all the signals."

Simon nodded. "Thanks."

"Michael!" the coach called from the field. "Michael Hensleigh!"

The kid slapped Simon on the back and took off for the baseball diamond.

"Good luck!" Simon called after him.

Simon watched as the kid began his tryout. To his surprise, he saw that Michael was going out for catcher, too.

Even worse, Michael was pretty good. And he never once landed on his butt!

I can't watch this, Simon decided. He turned away and headed for home. Mary had probably already left in disgust.

Bad enough the coach's son was good, Simon told himself miserably. *Now I have two guys looking to take my position!*

As if to match Simon's bleak mood, dark storm clouds began to gather in the late afternoon sky.

Shana dashed across the street just as the rain began to fall. She made it to the phone booth only to find an elderly woman using the telephone. Shana waited patiently while the woman finished her call.

The rain began to fall steadily. Soon it was pouring.

"All yours, sweetie," the woman called, hurrying by with an umbrella.

Shivering, Shana dialed Matt's number.

The line was busy. Again.

Shana pulled her collar up around her neck and rushed back across the street.

Lucy was still upset when Mary returned.

She was pacing back and forth in their

room, her pretty face pinched with worry.

"Where were you?" Lucy demanded when Mary entered the room.

"With Simon," Mary replied. "At the tryouts, remember?" She studied her sister.

"What's wrong?"

"Everything!" Lucy cried. "Dad won't do anything except to say I can't help Jimmy Moon and it's too dangerous to go anywhere near him!"

"Dangerous?"

Lucy nodded. "It's ridiculous."

"No, it isn't," Mary said.

"There are no drive-by shootings in Glenoak," Lucy said.

"Right," Mary shot back. "But what if Jimmy is high on something and driving his car? He could get into an accident, and if you were with him..."

"Enough with the doomsday scenarios!" Lucy cried.

"All I'm saying is that I agree with Dad. You should stay away from Jimmy."

Lucy sighed. "I will," she said simply.

"Promise!" Mary insisted.

"Okay, okay!" Lucy said, shaking her head. "I promise."

And I'm not lying, Lucy thought. *Even if I'm not exactly telling the truth, either.*

*   *   *

Matt was leaving his last class of the day when he heard someone call his name. He turned and stared into the throng of students rushing to and from their classes.

Then he spotted Connie. She was pushing her way through the crowded hallway. Her hair was wet from the afternoon cloudburst. And her eyes were flashing.

"Hey, rule-breaker!" Connie said when she finally caught up with him.

Matt gave her an innocent look. Connie didn't buy it.

"Amanda says she saw you kissing Charlotte last night," she said accusingly. "In the *middle* of the night. In the *middle* of our kitchen, where we cook our meals and wash our dishes."

"Actually, it was Charlotte who kissed *me*," he said defensively. "And it's not going to happen again."

"You're right!" Connie said, nodding. "Because you're moving *out!*"

"What?" Matt cried. "That's not fair. Why do I have to move out? Why can't Charlotte move out?"

Connie's eyes flashed again. "Because *you* are the problem. Not Charlotte."

For the first time, Matt could see the

hurt in Connie's eyes. *So that's what this is all about,* he thought.

"I'm not the problem," Matt said, more calmly. "And for your information, Amanda came on to me, too.

"As a matter of fact," he added, "you came on to me as well, if you'll recall."

"Oh," Connie replied coolly. "So high-and-mighty Matt Camden did *nothing* to get any of us to come on to him?"

Matt looked Connie in the eye. "No, I didn't."

Connie stamped her foot. "You know what you are?" she cried angrily. "You're... you're just...a *guy!*"

With that, she turned on her heel and walked away.

Matt leaned against the wall of the crowded hallway and scratched his head.

Mary came downstairs in her pajamas. She was surprised to see Simon sitting at the kitchen table.

"Hey, Simon," Mary said. "How did the rest of practice go?"

Simon looked away. "I know I'm good," he whispered.

Mary sat down next to him. "Sure. I know."

"But the coach's son is good, too. And there's this kid named Michael who's better than both of us, I think."

"Yeah," Mary nodded. "So you're *all* good."

"But only one or two of us can be the catcher, right?"

Mary sighed. "You're good, Simon."

"So what can I do to be even better?" he asked. "I need an edge."

Mary thought for a minute. "Look," she said finally. "Why don't you show the coach how much team spirit you have?"

"Team spirit? I don't get it."

"Yay, team!" Mary chanted, shaking her fists as if she were clutching pom-poms. "Rah-rah, team…Got it now?"

Simon nodded. "I guess so."

"Coaches love that kind of stuff," Mary continued. "That's what got me on varsity my first year in high school."

Simon jumped up, smiling broadly. "I have lots of team spirit!" he cried. "That's what I'm all about!"

"Good," Mary said, punching his arm playfully. "Now you're getting it."

"Hey," Simon went on, "I *live* for team spirit! It's even more important than being catcher."

Mary looked surprised.

"No, really," Simon insisted. "I just want to be on the team. I'd do anything. I'd even be the equipment manager if it meant I could be part of the team."

"Just show a little of that team spirit tomorrow, and you'll have it made," Mary said.

"You're right!" Simon's voice was filled with determination. "What I couldn't accomplish on the first day of tryouts, I'll do on the second."

"You're a shoo-in," Mary told him. "Now, how about a bowl of cereal?"

"Only if it's Wheaties," Simon said. "It's the Breakfast of Champions."

Lucy stood in front of the door to her father's study. Finally, her impatience got the better of her. She pushed it open.

Rev. Camden was sitting at his desk. He looked up when Lucy entered.

"Dad? I—"

"Listen," Rev. Camden interrupted her, "Sergeant Michaels hasn't returned my call yet. He's still unavailable."

Lucy frowned.

"But I just spoke to Jimmy Moon's parents," Rev. Camden added.

"And?"

"And Jimmy is all right."

Lucy whooped for joy.

"The police have dropped charges. I would guess that he'll be back in school tomorrow."

"That's it?" Lucy said, in disbelief.

"Yes," Rev. Camden replied. "That's as much as I feel comfortable telling you, yes."

"How about *my* comfort?" Lucy asked. "That explanation you gave me doesn't really make sense. How can a guy get arrested for smoking marijuana and then be back at school the next day?"

Rev. Camden raised one hand. "I don't think we know for sure that Jimmy was smoking marijuana," he said. "Maybe he was just sitting in the same car with some guys who were."

Lucy shook her head. "I saw them pass the joint back and forth. And the cop took a bag of something right out of Jimmy's pocket."

Lucy glared at her father. "So that's it?" she said finally.

"What else is there?"

"Fine," Lucy said angrily. "We both know that Jimmy is in a lot of trouble. And if you don't want to help him, I will."

She stormed out of the room.

Rev. Camden was about to follow her, but changed his mind. Instead, he picked up the phone and dialed.

Fifteen minutes later, he had finished his telephone conversation and returned to work on his Sunday sermon. While he re-read what he'd written, his thoughts turned bitter. He had a sinking feeling that this would be his last sermon at the church.

He worried about how he would support his family—especially now with the twins. Money was already tight. Without a job it would only get tighter.

Ruthie and Simon are too young to understand unemployment. And Matt, Mary, and Lucy still need my financial support.

Rev. Camden sighed. *What have I done wrong?* he asked himself. *Why is my congregation dissatisfied with my work?*

I must have done something, he decided. *If something was wrong at the church, and I didn't see it, it's my responsibility—and my fault—for not correcting it.*

His thoughts were interrupted by a knock at the study door.

Not again, Rev. Camden thought.

Matt stuck his head through the door.

"Well, well," Rev. Camden said. "The prodigal son returns."

"Ha, ha! Very funny," Matt replied.

"No, really," Rev. Camden said. "To what do we owe the pleasure of your company?"

He tapped his chin.

"Laundry?" he said. "No. Too late for that." He sat back in his chair and shook his head. "For the life of me, I can't think of a single reason for you to be here."

"I'm moving out," Matt said.

"I thought you had already done that."

"No, I'm moving out of the place I moved into."

"In less than twenty-four hours?" Rev. Camden said. "That's got to be a record. Something bad must have happened."

Matt shook his head. "Something happened, but it wasn't my fault. I didn't do anything."

Rev. Camden chuckled. "Sure you did," he said. "You moved in."

"So?" Matt was clearly confused.

"So take responsibility."

"For what?"

Rev. Camden sighed.

"For possibly not making the best decision in the world," he explained. "And for possibly making the wrong decision for the wrong reason."

Matt rolled his eyes. "Why is everyone blaming *me* for all this?" he cried.

"I don't know what 'all this' is, and I'm not blaming you."

"Well, it sounds like blame," Matt replied.

"No blame," Rev. Camden insisted. "I'm talking about taking responsibility, which is a very attractive quality in a person—even when you assume responsibility for something that is clearly and completely out of your control, and you don't even see it."

Matt shook his head. "Somehow I think you're talking about *you* now."

Rev. Camden smiled. "Son, you make me proud."

"Thanks, Dad," Matt said with a smile. "I'll try to take your advice."

Lucy was alone. Lying on her bed in the darkness, she considered her options.

Justin Dade.

The name ran through Lucy's mind over and over.

Though her conversation with Laura hadn't been very helpful, her friend had given her one vital piece of information—the name of the kid who'd run away when the police arrested Jimmy Moon. Laura said that Justin Dade had transferred from another school a few months ago.

She also said that he was dealing drugs.

But what do I do with that information? Lucy wondered. *Should I tell Dad? Go to the principal? The police?*

She wasn't sure.

Lucy understood that any action she took would probably lead nowhere. Her father had done nothing and continued to do nothing.

The police had arrived too late to arrest Justin, so they wouldn't go after him now.

And the principal would probably act the same way the police had—without evidence, there was nothing he could do.

So if nobody wanted to do anything to help Jimmy or stop the drug problem in their school, then it was up to her.

But what do *I do?* Lucy wondered. *I promised everyone that I wouldn't go near Jimmy Moon. But I didn't promise them I wouldn't do something.*

Lucy was certain there was only one course of action.

I'll confront Justin Dade and his friends myself, she decided.

Matt hung up the phone and sighed.

Still another attempt to reach Shana had failed. Her phone had rung, as usual, but this time the broken answering machine had never even picked up.

Matt would have been worried about her, except for the fact that the security guard at her apartment building had told him he'd seen Shana earlier that day.

Matt frowned. He was becoming confused about his feelings for Shana.

While he liked her a lot, Shana was hard to deal with sometimes. She often got moody and picked fights with him.

Even more troubling was how easy it was for him to forget Shana if circumstances were right.

After all, Matt thought guiltily, *I resisted Charlotte only for a minute. And I might have given in to Amanda just as easily.*

And Matt liked Connie, too. She was definitely on the right track nowadays, pulling her life together in a way few people could. Matt admired her for that.

Tomorrow he would have to go back and pick up his stuff. When he did, he would have to face Connie—and maybe Amanda and Charlotte, too.

Too bad it didn't work out, he thought

Suddenly, Matt realized that he'd moved in with Connie for selfish reasons. He'd kept telling himself that he was getting an apartment so Shana would feel more comfortable with their relationship.

But that wasn't the whole truth.

Matt *liked* the idea of being the only guy in three pretty and intelligent young women's lives. He loved the fact that they were vying for his time and attention.

Matt realized that he hadn't been honest—with any of them.

And he hadn't been honest with himself, either.

He cared for Shana. Yet just because they'd had a silly fight, he was willing to kiss a total stranger.

And that wasn't right.

Tomorrow I'm going to fix the messes I've caused, Matt decided. *Tomorrow I'm going to take responsibility for my actions.*

SIX

Matt was humming a tune on his way downstairs for breakfast the next morning. As he passed his sisters' room, Mary emerged. She was still in her pajamas and her hair was disheveled.

"Good morning!" Matt said cheerfully.

"What's so good about it?" Mary grumbled.

Matt smiled. "Nice morning. New day. Second chance at life!" he said merrily.

Mary rolled her eyes and went into the bathroom.

Matt found Simon in the kitchen.

His little brother was already dressed for school. He was tossing a baseball into the air and catching it—or trying to catch it.

"Whoa!" Matt cried when the baseball

bounced his way. "Remember what Mom said about playing ball inside the house."

When Simon went after the ball, his mitt bumped Ruthie's cup and milk splashed everywhere.

"How refreshing!" Ruthie cried.

Matt spent the next few minutes cleaning up his little sister. When he was finished, she actually hugged him.

"What was that for?" Matt asked.

Ruthie smiled. "That's for moving back into the house. Now we'll spend all our time together."

"I still have to go to school, remember?"

Ruthie nodded. "But without Shana, you'll be home a lot more."

"We'll see about that," Matt said.

"You are the best big brother in the world."

Matt was touched. He knelt down and looked into Ruthie's eyes. "Just because I'm seeing someone," he explained, "it doesn't mean I don't have time for you."

"That's the way it works out," Ruthie replied.

"I still like Shana," Matt told her. "And I still plan to see her. If we can ever get in touch again."

"Okay," Ruthie said with a frown.

"Now get ready for school," Matt said, pushing Ruthie out of the kitchen.

When she was gone, Matt turned back to Simon.

"So what's going on today?"

"Second day of tryouts," Simon replied. "But I don't know what we can cover today that we didn't cover yesterday."

"Maybe the coach wants to make sure nobody's performance yesterday—good or bad—was just a fluke," Matt said.

"What do you mean?" asked Simon.

"A guy might really be great, but could have had a bad day yesterday because he was nervous," Matt explained. "The coach is looking for consistency. He wants players who can do the same job every game."

"That's me," Simon said. "Mr. Consistency."

Just then, he dropped the baseball again. He went after it.

"You got *that* right," Matt muttered.

"Have you seen Mary?" Simon asked. "We should have been practicing a half-hour ago. Maybe I should call her…"

"Speaking of calls," Matt said, "if Shana calls today—"

"I know, I know!" Simon cried. "Tell

her you moved in with three women and you'll never see her again."

"Ha, ha," Matt said, his voice dripping with sarcasm. "Very funny."

He went off to retrieve his books and headed for school.

Matt was just out the door when the phone rang. Ruthie was the first to get there.

"I'll answer it!" she cried. No one seemed to hear. She picked up the receiver.

"Hello?" she said.

Simon rushed in.

"Is that Shana?" he demanded.

Ruthie covered the phone with her hand. "*No!*" she cried.

"Okay, okay!" Simon said. "I'll leave."

When he was gone, Ruthie put the phone to her ear again.

"Are you still on the line?" she asked.

"Hi," a voice said. "It's Shana. Is Matt there?"

"No," Ruthie replied. "I can't say that he is."

"That's just great!" Shana moaned, then began to cough. "Well, could you give him a message for me?"

Ruthie nodded, but said nothing.

"Hello?" Shana called.

"I'm here," said Ruthie.

Shana sighed. "Well, I wanted to let Matt know that I wouldn't be in school today because I'm sick from standing in the rain, trying to call him."

"Okay," Ruthie said.

"Tell him that I went to stay with my girlfriend Adele last night because I wasn't feeling well," Shana continued.

"Uh-huh."

"Tell Matt that I miss him, and I'm sorry I picked a fight with him."

Ruthie nodded.

"Though I suppose from his silence that Matt never wants to see me again."

"Okay," Ruthie said at last. "Good-bye." She hung up the phone.

Just then, Mrs. Camden passed through the room. "That wasn't Shana, was it?"

The little girl shook her head.

"Who was it?" Mrs. Camden pressed.

Ruthie shrugged. "I don't know," she lied. "Maybe it was a wrong number."

Lucy was dressed for school and heading downstairs when she was drafted for diaper duty by her mother.

Lucy held one twin while Mrs. Camden

changed the other. The baby on the bed struggled hard to squirm out of his mother's grip.

The expression on Lucy's face was one of impatience.

"I'll be done in a minute," Mrs. Camden said.

"Which one of us are you talking to?" Lucy asked.

Mrs. Camden glanced over her shoulder at Lucy.

"Don't be smart!" she demanded. "Be sweet to your brother. Babies pick up on everything. Including annoyance."

Lucy took a deep breath, then smiled down at the infant she cradled in her arms.

"Which one have I got?" she asked.

"That's Sam," Mrs. Camden said proudly.

Lucy studied Sam, then took a hard look at David. "They've changed so much in the past couple of weeks, I can't tell which one is which," she said.

Mrs. Camden chuckled. "Well, I can, because I'm their mother."

"So?" Lucy replied.

"So, one day you'll probably be a mother, too." Mrs. Camden turned and looked Lucy in the eye. "And you'll probably be a really good mother because you have such a strong sense of nurturing."

"You're saying babies," Lucy said. "But you're really talking about Jimmy Moon."

"Honey," Mrs. Camden began, "I know that you want to help Jimmy because he is in trouble, and the need to take care of others is a very natural instinct."

"Yeah." Lucy nodded. "But—?"

"But sometimes people want to nurture others more than they want to turn inward and nurture and take care of themselves."

Realization suddenly dawned on Lucy.

"Dad got to you, didn't he?" she cried. "He *always* gets to you."

Mrs. Camden sighed. "I assure you," she said, "I still have a mind of my own."

She finished with David's diaper and lifted him into her arms. The baby cooed and gurgled.

"I want to tell you something, Lucy," she said. "Woman to woman."

Lucy rolled her eyes.

"Please take everyone's advice right now. Let Jimmy Moon's family take care of Jimmy. And let Lucy take care of Lucy."

Mrs. Camden gazed into her daughter's eyes. "Please," she begged. "I don't want you to get hurt."

Lucy frowned. "You know something you're not telling me, don't you?"

"No," Mrs. Camden said. "But it's entirely possible that your father knows something he's not telling both of us."

She laid David in his crib. Then she took Samuel out of Lucy's arms. "All done," she announced.

"Thanks for the lecture," Lucy said over her shoulder as she walked away and went downstairs to the kitchen.

"Are you going to see Mary before school today?" she asked Simon.

"We're supposed to practice some throws," he said. "But time is running out."

"Tell her that I got a ride to school with Laura," Lucy said. She rushed out the door.

Lucy hurried across the yard and down the street. She didn't want anyone to catch her in the lie she'd just told.

In truth, Lucy was going to take public transportation to school. She wanted to get there early so she could head out to the dugout behind the high school.

She had a feeling that that was where she'd find Justin Dade.

And that was where Lucy was going to make her stand.

*　　*　　*

Matt was still in a great mood when he arrived on campus. Shana was in his literature class. He'd be sure to find her today.

Matt was ready to take full responsibility for the fight they'd had the other night. He was ready to promise to be more thoughtful and understanding. And he was ready to focus entirely on Shana and banish all other women from his life.

Matt knew that Shana was the right girl for him. And he was sure he was the right guy for her, too.

Matt trotted up the steps of Wylie Hall to his first class. Suddenly, he was stopped in his tracks by a hand pressing firmly against his chest.

He looked up to see Charlotte blocking his way. Her long hair was wild, and her green eyes were flashing.

"Well, well," she said. "Why didn't you tell me you were involved with Connie?"

"Me?" Matt stammered. "Involved with Connie?"

"Do you think I'm stupid or something?" Charlotte cried. "And I only find out after you came on to me in the kitchen!"

"Now wait a minute—" But Matt's mouth snapped shut.

He remembered the advice his father gave him. *Take responsibility*.

"All that stuff you and Connie came up with about not dating a roommate," Charlotte continued. "It was just a trick to get you—*her* boyfriend—into the apartment."

Charlotte's torrent of words came so fast that Matt was having trouble keeping up. People had begun to notice the very public scene.

This can't get any worse, Matt thought. Then it did.

"I thought you were going to keep away from Connie's guy!" a familiar voice cried.

Matt and Charlotte turned. Amanda was pushing through the crowd.

Charlotte put her hands on her hips. "Matt accosted *me*," she told Amanda with a toss of her head. "I was only being polite even talking to him."

"*You* stopped *me!*" Matt protested.

Amanda shook her finger in his face. "You should be ashamed of yourself, Matt Camden!" she cried.

The embarrassing confrontation was attracting a growing audience. Matt spotted his history professor in the crowd.

The girls began to yell at Matt—then at

each other. The crowd swelled.

Finally, Matt had had enough.

"Hold it!" he cried. "Everyone be quiet, please!"

Amanda and Charlotte stared at him.

"It's all my fault," Matt announced in a loud, clear voice.

The two women looked stunned.

"I know it was wrong," Matt continued, his voice contrite. "I wasn't thinking."

"You're right about *that*," Amanda said. Though she still sounded upset, much of her anger was gone.

Matt nodded. "I was only thinking of myself. And my selfish actions jeopardized the friendship you three women share."

"Things *were* fine until you showed up," Charlotte agreed.

"Which is why I'm moving out," Matt said. "It's the best thing for everyone."

"Do you have to move out?" Amanda cried.

"Stay," Charlotte urged. "We can work it out."

"I would only be imposing," Matt insisted.

"Are you sure?" Amanda asked, her voice pleading.

I've never been more sure of anything in

my entire life, Matt thought.

"It's the right thing to do," he said.

"But what about Connie?" Amanda asked. "Won't she be hurt?"

"Don't worry," Matt assured her. "I'll have a talk with Connie. She'll understand."

I hope.

"I want you to forget I ever came between you," Matt went on. "I want you to stay friends."

Amanda and Charlotte nodded. They didn't know quite what to say.

"I've got to go to class," Matt said finally. "But I'll drop by to speak with Connie later."

He paused.

"I'll miss you both and value the time we spent together. I hope you've learned something from my terrible mistake."

With a final wave of his hand, Matt went to class.

The women watched him go.

"What a great guy," Amanda sighed.

Rev. Camden left his desk and headed for Lou's office. He'd been at the church for an hour and hadn't seen a soul. Even worse, Rev. Camden hadn't seen the bulletin. He wondered if there was a problem.

At the deacon's office, Rev. Camden knocked, then opened the door.

He froze. Four startled, guilty-looking faces stared back at him from around Lou's desk. Two of them belonged to Lou and Sid. Beside them stood the church's organ player and Gene Tulley, the man from the copy shop that printed the bulletins.

"Oh…er…sorry," Rev. Camden stammered. "I didn't know you were busy."

On Lou's desk, Rev. Camden saw what looked like a mock-up of the church bulletin's front page. Lou quickly covered it with a hymnal.

"Can we help you, Eric?" he asked.

"I'm looking for Reverend Kelly's home number," Rev. Camden replied.

"Sure, Eric," Lou said. "I'd be happy to oblige. Let me finish up here first."

"No, it's okay," Rev. Camden replied. "I can see you're busy with…something. I'll just look up the number myself."

"Great," Lou said. "But if you can't find it, come by later and I'll give it to you."

Rev. Camden still lingered in the doorway.

"Is there anything else?" Lou asked.

"If you're working on the bulletin, I'd

be glad to help out," Rev. Camden offered.

Lou gave him a stern look. "We said we'd cover it," he replied. "And we will."

He got up and came around his desk. "Why don't you head home?" he suggested. "We've got to get back to work here."

With that, Lou gently shut the door.

It was early, but Lucy was already posted near Jimmy Moon's locker. While she waited, Lucy watched the other students. She wondered which of them might be using drugs. And which of them bought their drugs from Justin Dade.

Finally, Lucy saw Jimmy coming. When he saw her, he hesitated for a moment. Then he walked directly to his locker, ignoring her.

She stepped in front of him and blocked his way. Jimmy kept his eyes to the ground.

"I saw you in the parking lot yesterday," Lucy said, her voice sympathetic.

Jimmy snorted. "Who *didn't* see me?"

"So what happened?"

"What do you *think* happened?" Jimmy cried. "Nothing. I wasn't doing anything."

Lucy nodded, playing along. "I know," she whispered. "You were just in the wrong place at the wrong time."

Jimmy's stare became intense. "Yeah," he replied evenly. "That's exactly right."

"Look, Jimmy," Lucy said, touching his hand. "I want to say something."

Jimmy looked at Lucy's hand.

"I want to say that this is all my fault," she announced. "And I'm sorry."

Jimmy shook his head. "What are you talking about?" His voice was harsh.

"Everything," Lucy cried. "Even though we're not boyfriend and girlfriend anymore, we were once very close. At least, I *think* we were once very close."

She paused. Jimmy stared at her in utter confusion.

"I should have see that you were heading for trouble," Lucy continued. "I should have offered to help you. But I didn't then, so I am offering to help you now."

Jimmy remained silent.

"Would you say something, please?" Lucy begged. "I'm...I'm feeling so guilty."

"Why should *you* feel guilty?" Jimmy demanded. "*I* was the one who broke up with *you*. Remember?"

Lucy shook her head. "That was the first time," she insisted. "But the second time, I rejected you."

Jimmy didn't hear her. He was staring past Lucy. She turned, and her heart jumped. Standing fifty feet away were three punks.

One of them was Justin Dade.

Lucy's eyes met his, and Justin's lips curled into a snarl.

"It doesn't matter who rejected who!" Jimmy said, still looking past her. "I don't need your help."

"But—"

"No, Lucy," Jimmy said. "I don't."

Lucy was shocked at his tone.

"Get away from me!" Jimmy cried finally. "And stay away!"

Lucy rushed past Jimmy and down the hall, tears stinging her eyes. When she looked back, Lucy saw Jimmy Moon slapping hands with his bad-news buddies.

Justin Dade glanced in her direction and laughed.

SEVEN

Rev. Camden opened the front door just in time to see a huge ball of dirty towels roll down the stairs, coming right at him. He stepped back as the ball continued across the foyer and then hit the front door with a dull thump.

He looked up and saw his wife at the top of the steps.

"Sorry, honey," she called. "I didn't see you come in."

Rev. Camden smiled weakly.

Mrs. Camden gathered up the rest of the laundry and came down to greet him.

"Hi," Rev. Camden said, kissing her cheek.

"Do you mind you helping me for a second?" she asked.

"Not at all," he replied. "Set me to work."

Dropping his briefcase, Rev. Camden gathered up the wad of towels and walked with his wife to the laundry room.

"So," Mrs. Camden said after a moment. "Did you talk to Jimmy Moon's parents today?"

"I did," Rev. Camden said. "But I can't say a word about what was said."

Mrs. Camden's eyes were pleading.

"I'll just add that the Moons are worried about their son," said Rev. Camden. "But Jimmy is doing fine."

"That's a relief," said Mrs. Camden. But she sensed that he was still troubled.

"Something else happened today, didn't it?" she asked.

Rev. Camden shook his head, but Mrs. Camden knew he was not being honest.

"We've been married a long time—I know you, Eric Camden," she said. "I know when you're happy. I know when you're sad. And I know something is *definitely* bothering you."

Rev. Camden smiled weakly. He still said nothing.

"Pretend this is just like the Jimmy Moon situation," Mrs. Camden suggested.

"And just like the Jimmy Moon situation, you should tell me *some* of it."

Rev. Camden thought for a moment.

"If that doesn't work for you," she continued, "then give me the short version, and we'll go from there."

"The short version is that things are terrible," Rev. Camden said.

Mrs. Camden absorbed that news.

"Okay," she said softly. "Now let's try for the long version."

Rev. Camden leaned against the dryer. "Really terrible," he added.

"I can't help if you won't talk to me," Mrs. Camden insisted. She tossed the towels into the washer and closed the lid. Then she leaned against the machine, crossed her arms, and stared at Rev. Camden.

"No more games," she commanded. "Tell me what happened."

"I stopped by to see Lou on my way out the door," he said after a long pause. "I needed to get Reverend Kelly's phone number. He's the Moons' minister and—"

"Get to the important part," Mrs. Camden interrupted.

"I walked right into the middle of some sort of secret meeting," Rev. Camden said.

"Secret meeting?"

"Yes, a secret meeting," Rev. Camden repeated. "The kind of meeting that no one tells you about because it's a *secret*."

"Cut the sarcasm," said Mrs. Camden.

"Sorry," he replied.

"So what do you think they were doing?"

"I don't know."

"What did they *say* they were doing?"

"What are they supposed to say?" he demanded. "'Hey, Eric, as long as you're here, would you mind cleaning out your desk for the new guy?'" He paused for a moment. "Come to think of it, I can probably just keep the desk, since the new guy is having one delivered."

Mrs. Camden walked over to her husband and put her arm around his shoulder. "I realize the deacons seem to be taking a little more initiative than they usually do," she said. "But you don't know that any of this is true."

Rev. Camden nodded, slapped his knees, and then stood up.

"Anyway," he said, "I extricated myself as gracefully as I could. And then I called the Moons and spoke with them, and then I went down to the police station."

"Police station?"

"To talk to Sergeant Michaels about Jimmy's arrest," Rev. Camden explained. "And then do you know what happened?"

Mrs. Camden shook her head.

"*He* completely avoided me." Rev. Camden said, throwing up his arms. "I must have left twenty messages for him in the past two days, and he doesn't return any of my calls—I mean, what's going on?"

"So you didn't find out anything more about Jimmy's arrest?" Mrs. Camden asked.

"Not a thing."

"Well, I talked to Lucy this morning," Mrs. Camden said.

"And?"

"And I don't know how much good it did," she confessed.

"You know," Rev. Camden said, "I wanted to demand that she stay away from Jimmy Moon, but I was worried that she would do the opposite and run off to find him."

Mrs. Camden nodded.

"She may have done that anyway," he continued. "In fact, I'm sure she'll do it if she hasn't already."

"Do you know what will make you feel better?" asked Mrs. Camden.

"A generous trust fund and a full-time bodyguard for the kids?"

"*That* would work," she said, nodding. "But I've got something even better."

"And it is?"

"We have two beautiful kids upstairs that we can talk to who can't talk back!"

Rev. Camden laughed. "And they can't use the telephone!"

"And it will be years before they ask to borrow the car!" Mrs. Camden added.

Together, they ran up the stairs to visit the twins.

Lucy walked through the crowd that milled around school after the closing bell. Some of her friends called to her, but she ignored them all.

She walked to the back of the school, where the athletic fields and tennis courts were located. There were only a few people around. Most of them were running on the track.

Lucy walked past the joggers, past the bleachers, past the tennis courts, to the football field.

Lucy felt the cold sweat of fear on her neck and back. Her stomach quivered and her knees threatened to give out at any moment.

She was *very* afraid. More afraid than she'd ever been. But Lucy was also determined to master her fear.

"Hey, baby," a gruff male voice called from the shadows of the equipment shack. "Are you lookin' for something?"

Lucy halted. She strained her eyes, trying to pierce the darkness inside the dugout. Lucy could barely make out a black silhouette inside the tiny shack. She clutched her books to her chest and tried to control her breathing.

A figure emerged from the dimness. Lucy recognized him immediately.

It was Justin Dade.

Lucy groped for something to say, but she was suddenly struck dumb. She'd spent so much time planning this confrontation that she never thought about what she'd say when it actually happened.

"I...I saw you running from the police yesterday," she said at last. Her voice sounded strained.

Justin laughed. "Yeah, that was a kick," he said, taking a step toward her. Lucy quickly stepped back. Justin leaned against the walls of the shack.

"So what are you shopping for?" he asked with a smirk. He thrust his hands into the pockets of his black jeans and stared at Lucy, waiting for a reply.

"I'm not shopping," Lucy said. "I came here to give you a message."

Justin stood up straight. "A message? Sounds pretty heavy."

"I want you to leave Jimmy Moon alone."

Justin looked confused. "Leave *Jimmy* alone?" he repeated. "I don't even want that little snot around. So how can *I* leave *him* alone?"

Lucy's eyes flashed. She was angry now, despite her fear.

"You know what you did to him," she said. Her voice was low, clear, and authoritative. Justin blinked, clearly taken aback.

"What's Jimmy to you, anyway?" he retorted, taking a step closer.

"Stay away from me," Lucy demanded. "And stay away from Jimmy, too."

Justin threw back his head and laughed. "Jimmy should stay away from *us*," he said. "That leech is always hanging around. We should charge him for the privilege of staying in our presence."

Lucy glared at the boy.

"What's he to you?" Justin demanded.

"He's my—" Lucy hesitated. "He's my friend," she said.

Justin snickered.

"He used to be your *boyfriend*," he fired back. "Until he dumped you."

"That's not true," Lucy insisted. "I dumped him. The second time, anyway."

"Revenge for the first dump?" Justin asked. "The one where *he* dumped *you?*"

"It wasn't like that."

"Maybe Jimmy was tired of you butting into his life," Justin added.

"Being a friend is not butting in," Lucy protested. "I care about Jimmy, and I don't want to see him hurt."

"I'll tell him you came by," Justin said. "Now run off and play with the other nice girls."

Lucy stood her ground until she sensed movement behind her. She turned to see several other punks approaching the shack from across the field.

"I've got to go," Lucy said.

"You sure you've gotten everything you came for, little girl?" Justin asked.

Lucy looked over her shoulder and saw the other guys were getting very close.

Without another word, she turned on her heel and walked away. As she went back toward school, she controlled her pace, trying to remain calm. Her path brought her close to the punks.

"Where you going, girl?" one called.

Lucy continued on, ignoring them. She walked slowly and deliberately toward the school. She changed direction when she got there and rounded the corner. As soon as she was out of sight of the gang, her self-control disappeared. Lucy took off in a burst of speed, running as fast as she could. She wanted to get as far away from Justin Dade and his loser friends as fast as possible.

Shana sneezed. She put her hand on her forehead but couldn't detect a fever. She still felt very weak, but she managed to roll over on the sofa and sit up. She felt a bit better than she had the day before—which was to say she felt miserable—but at least she didn't feel like she was on her last legs anymore.

She looked around the unfamiliar apartment, grateful that her friend Adele had invited her over. She didn't like being alone when she didn't feel well, and her own apartment seemed huge and empty since her fight with Matt.

It's my fault, she thought. *I wouldn't blame Matt if he never talked to me again.*

The apartment was quiet—too quiet. Shana hated the feeling of loneliness that she had had for the past few days. But unfortunately, she was alone again. Adele had gone to class, agreeing to pick up Shana's assignments from her professors for her. But Adele wasn't back yet, and Shana was feeling restless.

She blew her nose and tossed the tissue into the trash. She checked the time.

It was nearly four o'clock in the afternoon. Most classes at Crawford were over. She knew that Matt's final class had ended more than an hour ago. She picked up Adele's phone and called the Camdens'.

Ruthie was in the living room, dressing one of her favorite dolls in a festive outfit. When the phone rang, she looked around for someone to answer it.

"Mom!" she called. But Mrs. Camden and Rev. Camden were upstairs with the twins. So the little girl rolled her eyes and answered the telephone.

"Hello?" she said.

"Hi, Ruthie! Remember me?" Shana said, trying to sound happy.

"What's wrong with your voice?" asked Ruthie.

"I have a cold," she explained. "I think I might be getting laryngitis, too."

"Lauren who?" Ruthie replied.

"No," said Shana. *"Laryngitis."*

"What's that?"

"Well," Shana continued patiently, "it's when you are so sick you have trouble talking."

"If you're having trouble talking, then why do you keep calling me up?" Ruthie asked, confused.

"I'm not calling you," Shana replied. "I'm calling Matt."

Ruthie was quiet for a moment. "Matt moved out," she said finally.

"Moved out?" Shana cried. Then she broke down into a spasm of coughing.

"Is there anything else?" Ruthie asked.

"No!" Shana choked. "Don't hang up—"

"Bye," Ruthie said politely before she hung up the phone.

On the other end of the line, Shana screamed out her frustration and pounded the sofa with her fists. She felt helpless. She had called Matt a half-dozen times—

but if she didn't get a busy signal, then Ruthie always answered the phone.

Suddenly, it dawned on Shana that Matt might not be getting the messages she'd been leaving with the little girl. Perhaps, Shana thought, innocent little Ruthie might have an agenda of her own.

Simon stretched out for another pitch, but the ball brushed his glove and bounced into the backstop. It rolled to a stop in the dust. Simon grabbed the ball and shot it back to the pitcher. The throw was straight, and the pitcher caught it easily. Simon smiled under his face mask.

Behind the backstop, Mary watched her brother warm up. She was happy to see an improvement in his form. She was also pleased to see that some of Simon's self-confidence had returned.

While she watched, the pitcher fired another ball his way.

This one was low, but Simon made a good catch in the dirt.

"Nice scoop, Camden!" Mary called. She turned and saw the coach watching Simon. He wrote something on his clipboard.

"Great day for some ball," Mary said,

trying to sound casual.

"Beautiful," the coach agreed. "Outfield grass was a little wet when we started, but it's drying up nice."

"Don't want everybody slipping all over the place," Mary observed.

The coach chuckled. "Some of these kids do that anyway."

Mary chuckled back. "So how's the team shaping up?" she asked.

The coach lifted his cap and scratched his head. Then he glanced at Mary. "Today is the hardest part of the season, as far as I'm concerned," he remarked. "Who to keep and who to cut. It's a tough call."

"That *is* tough," Mary agreed.

"If it was up to me, I'd keep almost all of them," the coach said. "But the school only allows a certain number of students on the roster."

"Yeah, good luck," Mary added.

The coach nodded and wrote something else down on his clipboard. Mary made a move to depart, then paused.

"I'm not just saying this because he's my brother, but I don't think I've ever met anyone with as much team spirit as Simon."

The coach stopped writing and looked at Mary. "Is that right?" he replied.

Mary nodded. "He is so psyched just to be working out with you and the guys on the team," she continued.

"You sure?" asked the coach.

"Definitely," Mary said. "And Simon doesn't even have to be catcher, if that doesn't work out."

Mary leaned toward the coach and whispered, "Do you know what he said to me yesterday?"

The coach shook his head.

"He said that the most important thing was just being part of the team," Mary said. "He even told me that he would be thrilled to be the equipment manager! That's how much he wants to be a part of things!"

"Did he really say that?"

Mary nodded enthusiastically.

The coach looked at Simon. Simon glanced Mary's way at just that moment. He smiled and gave his sister a wave.

"Thanks for the information, Camden," the coach said.

"It's my pleasure," she replied. "Anything for the team."

When the coach walked away, Simon looked at his sister again. This time Mary gave him a thumbs-up.

Simon's grin was so wide it threatened to escape his face mask.

Shana peeked out from under the comforter when she heard a key in the lock. Adele breezed into the room a moment later with a solicitous smile on her face.

"How do you feel, Shana?" she asked.

Shana sat up. "Okay, I guess."

Adele laid her cool hand on her friend's brow. "You still have a fever," Adele announced.

Shana nodded weakly. "But I feel better."

"That's good," Adele replied, "because Professor Johnson gave you a whopper of an assignment."

Shana rolled her eyes in disgust. "Great!" she muttered.

"But don't worry," Adele added. "I managed to score you some notes and even the reference book you'll need."

"Thanks," Shana replied gratefully. "You're a pal, Adele."

"That's what I'm here for."

Adele gave Shana her school material

and explained the assignment. Shana took some notes, then set the books aside.

"I'm too sad to work right now," said Shana.

"I understand," Adele replied, her eyes shifting.

Shana sensed that her friend was hiding something.

"Did you run into Matt today?" Shana asked.

Adele turned away.

"I didn't actually *see* him," Adele answered after a pause.

"But..." Shana probed.

Adele sighed, and then she looked at Shana. Her eyes were full of pity.

"But?" Shana repeated, this time more insistently.

"But I—I heard some things," Adele whispered softly.

"Heard things?" Shana cried. "What kind of things?"

Adele sighed again. "I heard that Matt had a fight with two girls in Wylie Hall."

"That doesn't sound like Matt at all!" Shana cried.

"It *was* him, though," Adele insisted. "I heard the whole story from Pamela Hensleigh."

Shana rolled her eyes. "Pamela Hensleigh is a ditz."

Adele nodded. "But she's a ditz who knows all the gossip at Crawford."

"What did Pamela say?" Shana asked in a small voice.

Suddenly, Adele's eyes lit up with excitement.

"Pamela said that Matt had a very public confrontation with two girls named Charlotte and Amanda—" she continued.

"I've never heard of them," Shana interrupted.

"Pamela told me that they were arguing about Matt making out with one of them," Adele continued, ignoring Shana. "Or maybe it was *both* of them."

Shana was upset, but she had to hear more.

"The two girls even brought up a third girl," Adele giggled. "Someone named Connie, I think."

That's the girl Matt took to his high school prom, Shana recalled.

At that moment, Shana felt sick all over again. Adele continued to dish up the dirt, oblivious to her friend's troubled expression.

"One of the girls even said that Matt was Connie's boyfriend!"

Shana gulped. That was news to her—bad news!

Could Matt have been playing me for a fool all along? Shana wondered. *This doesn't sound like the Matt I know, but...*

Shana threw off the blanket.

"I've got to find him," she said. "I've got to find out what's going on."

Adele grabbed her friend before she could fall back down onto the sofa.

"You can hardly walk!" Adele said. "Forget about Matt. He's no good for you, anyway."

"You're right," Shana murmured. "I don't feel so good."

"You still have a temperature," Adele declared. "Lie down and I'll fetch the thermometer."

EIGHT

Matt unlocked the apartment door. Inside it was dark with the gloom of early evening. A single reading lamp glowed next to the sofa in the living room.

Matt bumped something with his foot.

A cardboard box had been set in the entranceway. It contained all of the stuff he'd brought over the other night.

Matt crossed to the living room.

Connie was on the couch. The light made her face look pale and sad.

Matt sat down next to her. Connie ignored him.

"Thanks for packing my things," he said softly.

Connie shifted on the sofa.

"This whole mess was my fault. I should have been the one packing."

Connie faced Matt.

"So you *did* kiss Charlotte?" she said.

"Let's just say that I didn't *not* kiss her," he said. "That's not the same thing to me, but it probably is to you. Anyway, who kissed who is not the problem."

"Oh?" Connie shot back.

"The problem is that living with three women is probably not going to work out for me," Matt confessed. "I'm just sorry I didn't realize that before I upset everyone."

Connie was surprised by Matt's response. "Well, thanks for apologizing," she said. "And even though we're not roommates, maybe we can still be friends."

"I'd like to be friends," Matt replied.

Connie laughed. "According to Charlotte and Amanda, we're *more* than friends."

"Listen," Matt said, "there's something I have to explain…"

"You don't have to explain anything," Connie insisted. "We were never a couple, and I don't think we ever *will* be."

"That's not true," Matt responded. "I am very attracted to you."

Connie laughed again. "Thanks."

"It's the truth."

"So does that mean I should be expecting your call?"

Matt looked down, trying to avoid Connie's eyes. "There's something I should tell you," he began. "Maybe I should have told you sooner, but..."

Connie waved him off. "I already know about the other girl," she announced.

Matt blinked. "You do?"

"Pamela Hensleigh told me all about her. You're seeing someone named Shana."

"Yes," Matt replied. "I should have told you when we met at the bulletin board."

"Why?" Connie said. "We were friends and potential roommates, not boyfriend and girlfriend."

"But I thought—"

"That just because I tried to kiss you, all I wanted was a boyfriend, right?"

Matt nodded. "Something like that."

"Well, forget it!" Connie said. "I'm going to concentrate on school right now. I don't have time for a boyfriend. I had too many of those in high school. Now it's time to play catch-up."

Matt felt relieved.

"You'd better go," Connie said. "Charlotte and Amanda will be home soon.

And I sure don't want another scene."

"Neither do I!" Matt laughed.

"Thanks for everything," Connie said.

"No," Matt replied. "Thank *you*."

He picked up the box. "I guess I'll see you around."

Connie waved him away. "Get out of here, Camden!"

With one last look, Matt left the apartment.

When he was gone, Connie's bright smile was gone, too, and her brave face had vanished.

Her eyes were moist with tears.

Lucy stared at the ceiling. The memory of her confrontation with Jimmy—and Justin Dade—raced through her mind.

It had been awful. But Lucy knew that she would do it again if it could help Jimmy Moon.

Lucy considered her next move. *Just because a friend doesn't want your support doesn't mean he doesn't need it.*

And Jimmy Moon definitely needs some kind of help.

He's as scared of those guys as I am, Lucy realized. *But if he's so afraid, why does he go near them at all?*

What kind of hold do those guys have over Jimmy? Lucy wondered.

Matt walked into the house and set the box down on the kitchen table.

Then he crossed to the refrigerator, where the family left notes and messages. There was a message for Simon from some kid named Michael and a note reminding Mary that she had a field trip next week.

But there was nothing for Matt from Shana.

Ruthie greeted him at the top of the stairs. She was holding her favorite book of bedtime stories.

"Hey, big brother!" Ruthie said.

"Hey, yourself," Matt replied, running a hand through her curly hair. "Aren't you up a little late?"

"Yeah." She nodded. "But since you're moving back in with us, you could read me a story."

"Who told you that I was moving back in?" Matt asked.

"Mom," Ruthie replied. "Mary said that you couldn't handle one girl, let alone three. What did she mean by that?"

Matt looked toward Mary's room and frowned. "I don't know. But I think I'll have a talk with her in the morning."

"What about my story?"

Matt sighed. "You know that I'd *like* to—"

Ruthie's smile disappeared. "But?"

"*But* I spent half the day arguing and trying to fix my life. Now I've got a paper to write. It's due tomorrow."

He scratched Ruthie's chin. "I'm sorry," he said. "Maybe another night, okay?"

Ruthie looked up at him doubtfully.

"Honest," Matt promised her. "I'm back now, and I'll read you stories for the next month if you want me to."

Ruthie beamed. "It's a deal!" she cried.

Matt patted her shoulder and went to his room. He sat down at the desk and went to work.

Lucy fled her room, anxious to escape the thoughts that ran through her mind in an endless loop. She needed to talk to somebody. But Mary had gone out, and Matt was busy studying. Lucy wasn't sure that her father or mother would understand.

She threw on her robe and raced downstairs. She walked through the dimly lit living room toward her father's study. When she got there, she saw that the door was open and the light was on. Her father was hard at work, typing something on his computer. She reached out her hand to knock on the door, but changed her mind.

Lucy headed for the kitchen.

Simon lay on his bed. But sleep would not come.

Simon knew the reason for his insomnia. Tomorrow afternoon, the names of the students who made the baseball team would be posted.

He had pulled out all the stops to get a spot on the team. He'd practiced, he'd gone to the tryouts, and he'd even used his big sister as an endorsement.

But Simon realized now that it was all about how well he played.

I'm pretty good, he reasoned. *But is that enough?*

Simon thought about the other kids going out for catcher. The coach's son was not bad. And Michael was good.

He reached down to give his dog, Happy, a pat.

"You'll love and respect me even if I don't make the team, won't you, Happy?"

The dog yelped in reply.

"I hope I can still respect myself."

Simon rolled over, pulled the blankets up to his chin, and tried to sleep.

Lucy found her mother at the kitchen table. A baby was cradled in her arms.

"I'm trying to get Sam here to go to sleep," Mrs. Camden explained. "He's pretty restless tonight, and I didn't want him to wake David."

Lucy nodded and sat down.

"I guess we're all pretty restless tonight," she said.

Mrs. Camden looked at her daughter. "Are you all right?"

Lucy shrugged. "What difference does it make?"

Mrs. Camden frowned. "You know I hate it when you answer a question with another question. And it makes a big difference."

"Not to Dad," Lucy said miserably. "He's sitting in his study, working on his sermon, like he could change anything with a few words on a Sunday morning!"

Mrs. Camden stared at Lucy, surprised at her daughter's bitterness.

"Your father has a job to do," Mrs. Camden replied. "A very important job."

"Oh, yeah?" Lucy shot back, startling the baby. "He *could* be doing something important, like reaching out to Jimmy Moon. But he does absolutely nothing."

Mrs. Camden soothed the rattled baby. When he was calm, she turned to Lucy.

"Your dad and I really do care about you, and we care about your friends, too. Past and present."

Lucy rolled her eyes. "Right."

"But sometimes your dad just can't help, for whatever reason. And I honestly think he doesn't really know what's going on with Jimmy Moon or his family."

"Why not?" Lucy cried. "Everybody in school knows! The whole world knows!"

"Everybody *thinks* they know what's going on," Mrs. Camden said.

I do, Lucy thought. But she said nothing. Instead, she silently rocked in her chair, fighting back tears.

"Look, Lucy," Mrs. Camden begged. "Please keep your distance from Jimmy Moon and his friends."

Lucy nodded but said nothing.

"I'm not asking you," her mother added firmly. "I'm *telling* you."

Again, Lucy nodded.

"It's very important that you just trust

me on this one, okay?"

Samuel sobbed again. Mrs. Camden directed her attention to the baby.

Lucy rose and left the kitchen.

Shana awoke feeling much better, considering she'd spent the night on her friend's sofa again.

Her fever had broken, and her aches and pains were pretty much gone.

On the coffee table, Shana found a note from Adele.

Had to go to class, the note read. *But I left some orange juice and fruit in the refrigerator. Make yourself at home. Love, Adele.*

Shana poured herself a glass of juice and grabbed a banana.

As she ate, she paged through her class notes. The test wasn't until Monday. That gave her a few days to worry about it.

Shana rose and stretched when she was done with breakfast. She cleaned up the living room so that Adele wouldn't find a mess when she got home.

While she cleaned up, Shana recalled Adele's advice.

"Don't get paranoid," Adele had said. "Not until you talk to Matt and find out what's really going on."

That was good advice, Shana decided. *Now it's time to put it into practice.*

She dialed the Camdens' number.

Ruthie rushed across the living room and grabbed the phone before anyone else—especially Matt—could answer.

"Hello?" she said cautiously.

"Hello, Ruthie," Shana said. "Is Matt there?"

Ruthie looked around the room before replying.

"He's here," she said finally. "But he's working on a paper. Can I take a message?"

Shana sighed. "So Matt *is* there?"

"He *might* be," Ruthie said. "But he might *not* be. I can't be sure."

"Well, then, I guess there's only one way to find out," Shana said.

"What's that?"

But Shana had already hung up.

"How rude!" Ruthie exclaimed. "She didn't even say good-bye."

Matt finished reading over his paper. It was good, but uninspired.

It will just have to do, he decided.

Matt stuffed the paper into his folder.

Just then, the doorbell rang. Matt

bolted down the steps in time to spot Ruthie running to the door.

"I'll get it," she declared.

The little girl opened the door a few inches and peered out of the crack.

"Who is it?" she asked.

"It's Shana."

Matt threw the door open.

He and Shana stared at each other for a moment, then they both cried out at once, "I've been trying to call you!"

They laughed.

Then Matt noticed Ruthie trying to slink away. He grabbed her by her backpack.

"Hold it, kiddo," he said. "I've got a few questions for you."

"What do I know?" Ruthie insisted. She tried to squirm away, but her big brother was way too strong for her.

Shana looked at Matt. "So you didn't move out."

"Well, actually I *did*, but now I'm back."

Shana blinked.

"It's a long story," Matt added. "I'll give you the scoop later."

"Ruthie gave you my messages, right?"

Matt shook his head and looked down at the little girl. Ruthie still struggled against his grip.

"Did Shana leave a message with you?" he demanded.

Ruthie stopped fighting. "Yes," she replied, shamefaced.

Matt released her.

"Actually," Shana added, "I left more than one message."

Ruthie nodded. "Two, I think."

"Two!" Matt cried. "Why didn't you tell me Shana called? You would have saved us both a lot of trouble."

"I'm sorry," Ruthie said. "I thought it would be better for me if you didn't know."

"Better for *you*?" Matt said. "Why?"

Ruthie crossed her arms. "Mary and Lucy have each other, and Simon has the twins."

She looked up at Matt. "That just leaves the two of us, right?"

"I guess," Matt said.

"Except that you're always too busy," Ruthie continued. "If you aren't visiting Shana, then you're at college. If you're not at college, you're moving out!"

"I see," Matt said.

Then he pointed Ruthie in the direction of the living room. "Go in there and wait for me," he said.

Ruthie trudged off, leaving Matt and Shana alone in the foyer.

"I'm going to have to handle this," Matt said, nodding in Ruthie's direction.

Shana understood immediately. "Sure," she said.

"What do you say we get together this weekend and talk?" Matt suggested.

"We'll definitely have to get together in person to talk," Shana said. "My answering machine is broken, and I don't have the money to buy a new one."

"We don't have the money to get an old one," Matt said. "All we have is Ruthie's Answering Service, and you know how reliable *that* is."

They both laughed. The whole situation was actually kind of funny now—now that they were together again.

"So how about Saturday night?" Matt offered.

"Great!" Shana said, throwing her arms around him. They kissed for a few moments, then slowly parted.

"We'll go out somewhere," Matt declared. "I mean," he added quickly, "if you want to."

"Actually," Shana confessed, "after two days and a night at Adele's, my apartment sounds just fine."

"Well," Matt said, glancing at his watch, "I've got to talk to Ruthie and get ready for classes."

"Me too," Shana added. "I've got to catch up on the days I missed."

"See you later, then."

"Right!" Shana gave him a huge smile, warm and inviting. She peeked around the corner, into the living room.

"Good-bye, Ruthie," she called.

After Shana was gone, Matt walked into the living room. Ruthie was sitting quietly on the sofa, waiting for his lecture.

"I'm sorry," she said immediately. "Please don't be mad at me."

To her surprise, Matt smiled. "I'm not mad," he told her. "Not anymore."

Ruthie gave him a doubtful look. "You should be mad," she said. "I did a bad thing."

"Well, maybe you did," Matt admitted. "But I guess you did it for a good reason."

"I did?"

"Sure," Matt continued. "You wanted to spend more time with me. That's a good thing, because I like spending time with you, too."

"You do?"

"Sure!" Matt exclaimed. "I'll prove it to you."

"How are you going to do that?" Ruthie asked.

"Simple," Matt replied. "I'm going to pick you up after school today and we'll spend the whole afternoon together."

"Yippee!" Ruthie clapped her hands and jumped up and down.

"So get to school," Matt commanded. "And work hard. We're going to have lots and lots of fun later."

Suddenly, Ruthie frowned. "But what about tomorrow?" she said. "And the next day? And the day after that?"

"Look," Matt said, "I know I've been neglecting you. I'm going to make more time for you now, okay? I promise."

"Okay," Ruthie said, hugging him.

"You know what I'm going to do for you?" she asked.

"What?"

"I'm going to start giving you all of your messages," Ruthie said.

Then she ran off to catch the school bus.

NINE

"Hey, Camden!" Maxwell cried. "What are you doing this weekend?"

"Saturday is the first day of baseball practice," Simon informed him. "I'll be on the field with the rest of my team."

"Yeah, right," Maxwell laughed. "I watched the tryouts, remember? You don't have a chance."

"We'll just see about that!" Simon turned and walked down the hall.

"Hey, Simon! Wait up!"

Simon turned to see Michael running up to him.

"Man," Michael gasped. "I thought I'd never catch up to you."

"Well, you found me," Simon said. "What do you want?"

"I didn't get to talk to you after the try-outs," Michael said. "That was a great catch you made in the dirt!"

"It's easy," Simon lied.

"I wish you'd teach me!"

Simon was suddenly suspicious. "Why? So you can be a better catcher than me?"

"Well," Michael grinned, "so I can be a better catcher, anyway."

"Let's walk," Simon suggested. The boys proceeded through the halls.

"Actually," Simon confessed, "I had trouble with saves for a long time. But my sister taught me how to catch the really tough throws. She's a varsity champ."

"Yeah?" Michael replied. "You're lucky. My sister goes to college and talks on the telephone. That's about it."

"Does she go to Crawford?"

Michael nodded.

"My brother goes there, too," Simon said. "Maybe he knows her."

Their conversation was interrupted by kids rushing for the bulletin board. Simon and Michael hurried after them.

"What's going on?" Simon asked.

One of the kids Simon recognized from tryouts spoke. "They just put up the list."

Simon's heart froze.

The kid laughed. "You're on it!"

Simon grinned. "You're kidding!"

Michael and Simon pushed their way through the crowd.

"You go, girl!" Maxwell called to Simon. He and his pals exploded with laughter.

A moment later, Simon reached the bulletin board and scanned the list.

When he saw his name, Simon's jaw dropped.

Mary's day at school had proceeded without incident until her gym teacher, Mrs. Kelso, caught up with her in the hallway.

"Mary," Mrs. Kelso said, "come with me."

Startled, Mary followed her. Students whispered as they watched them go.

Mary waited until they were away from prying eyes before she spoke. "What's the matter?"

"Your brother is on the phone that's in the P.E. office."

Mary was suddenly filled with fear.

"He sounds a little frantic," Mrs. Kelso continued.

"Did Matt say it was an emergency?" Mary asked.

"Actually, I think it's your younger brother Simon."

Mary breathed a little easier.

Mrs. Kelso quickly ushered her into the P.E. office. Equipment hung everywhere. At one end of the room, a phone sat on an otherwise empty desk. "There you go," Mrs. Kelso said. She left Mary alone.

Mary lifted the receiver. "Hello?"

"Hello?" Simon said. "Is this Mary?"

"Simon!" she cried impatiently. "Don't you recognize my voice?"

"I just wanted to be sure I was speaking to the right person," Simon continued. "I'd be too ashamed to talk to anyone else."

"What happened?"

"Guess," Simon replied.

"What do you mean *guess?*" Mary said. "Just tell me what's the matter or I'll hang up right now."

"Nothing's the matter," Simon said sarcastically. "Except that I'm the baseball team's new *equipment manager!*"

The last two words were screamed out. Mary held the phone away from her ear.

"Gee!" Simon shouted. "Where do you suppose the coach ever got the idea?"

"What are you yelling at me for?" Mary cried. "All I did was put in a good word for you."

"Do you know what the equipment manager's job *is?*" he demanded. "He has to lug all the equipment out to the field every day, carry loads of the team's steaming, putrid laundry to the laundry truck after every single game, rake the dirt around the infield—"

"Look, I'm in school," Mary said, interrupting him. "Can we talk about this later?"

"Can we talk about this *later?*" Simon repeated. "How about if you talk to the coach? Because if it weren't for your big fat mouth and your advice about team spirit, I'd probably be outside playing baseball right now instead of hiding, too ashamed to show my face in school ever again!"

"All right! Fine!" Mary shouted back at him. "I'll talk to the coach. I don't know what I'm supposed to say to him, but—"

Simon had already hung up.

Mary sighed. She turned around to see a tall, gawky freshman with braces pushing a huge canvas cart through the double doors. She was having a hard time of it. Mary held the doors open.

"Thanks," the girl said.

Mary suddenly recognized her.

"Hey!" she said. "You're the equipment manager for varsity basketball, aren't you?"

"Yeah," the girl replied shyly. She was almost as tall as Mary, but walked with a slight stoop.

"I've seen you throw hoops," Mary remarked. "You're good. Except that you dribble a little low. Stop by after practice and I'll give you a few pointers."

"Gee," the girl said brightly. "Thanks."

"No," Mary replied. "Thank *you*. I never realized the cruddy stuff you equipment managers have to put up with."

Simon cut study hall and was hiding under a fire escape. He was waiting for the school to clear out before he skulked home.

"Equipment manager," he muttered.

Though the fire escape was a popular hangout during school hours, not many people came there on a Friday.

So Simon was surprised to see someone come around the corner. He was even more surprised that it was Michael.

"I saw you made the team," Mike said. His tone was sincere.

"Yeah," Simon said miserably. "Did you?"

Michael nodded. "I'm the catcher."

"Congratulations," Simon said, trying not to sound bitter.

"I'm not too happy about it," Michael said. He sounded depressed.

Simon blinked in surprise.

"Who am I kidding?" Michael cried. "My dad made me practice for six solid weeks and I'm still no good."

He looked at Simon, his face stricken. "I'll choke in the first inning of the first game."

"Are you crazy?" Simon replied. "You were even better than the coach's son. And he was great!"

Mike shook his head. "I don't think so. You're the one who's got the moves."

"It's not about moves," Simon confessed. "I got those from watching television. Moves are just...showmanship."

Michael looked puzzled.

"Saving in the dirt, stuff like that. It's just theatrics," Simon explained.

"Really?"

"Sure," Simon continued. "It's pretty obvious to me what happened. The coach saw your potential."

Mike shook his head.

"Really," Simon insisted. "He's coached kids for years. Don't you think he can recognize talent?"

"I'm only going to stay on the team if you are," Mike announced.

"Oh, no," Simon said. "You can't hold me to that."

"You *have* to be there," Mike insisted. "I won't be able to do it without you. You've got to show me the moves, Simon."

"I'll think about it," Simon said.

Rev. Camden sat across his desk from Mr. and Mrs. Moon. The late afternoon sun streaming through the window did little to lighten the tone of the meeting. For everyone concerned, it was an uncomfortable scene.

"You know that my daughter considers Jimmy to be her friend," Rev. Camden said. "She's concerned about him."

"Well," Mr. Moon said, shifting uncomfortably in his chair, "I think our boy has been scared straight by his arrest."

"Not that he was doing anything wrong to begin with," Mrs. Moon added.

Rev. Camden blinked. "So you think it's true that Jimmy wasn't using marijuana?"

Mr. and Mrs. Moon exchanged nervous glances. Both of them avoided Rev. Camden's gaze.

"Well," Mrs. Moon said finally, "it sounds better than the alternative."

"And the important thing is that the police believed it," Jimmy's father added. Mrs. Moon nodded in agreement.

"Did it ever occur to either of you that the police might have made some kind of deal with Jimmy?" Rev. Camden asked.

Mr. Moon looked surprised. "A deal?"

His wife shook her head. "Jimmy isn't some kind of drug lord," she said. "What could he possibly offer the police?"

"I'm not sure," Rev. Camden replied. "But I'm sure that Jimmy was offered leniency in exchange for becoming a teen informant."

Mr. and Mrs. Moon paled.

"That's crazy," the woman insisted. "Wouldn't something like that require our permission?"

But Rev. Camden shook his head. "Not in this state," he explained. "All that is required is the consent of the minor."

Now Mr. Moon's face was flushed with anger. "Well, I don't like the sound of that!" he cried. "It sounds dangerous."

"It is," Rev. Camden replied. "Of course, many law enforcement personnel feel it is the only way to catch dealers who sell to kids in and around schools."

"And these...children," Mrs. Moon said. "They *want* to do this?"

Rev. Camden sighed. "When the alternative is going to jail or a juvenile detention center, yes."

Mrs. Moon was on the verge of tears.

"So what do we do, Reverend?" Mrs. Moon asked, her voice choked with emotion.

"I think it's best that you ask Jimmy what really happened with the police," Rev. Camden said gently. "Confront him. Tell him of your suspicions. And do it today. The sooner, the better."

Just then, the telephone rang. Rev. Camden spoke for a minute, then hung up.

"I'm sorry," he said, rising. "I hate to cut this short, but I need to pick Lucy up."

"We understand," Mr. Moon said, rising.

"Of course," Mrs. Moon added. "We understand perfectly."

Lou suddenly breezed through the door and into Rev. Camden's office.

"Oh, I am *so* sorry," Lou said. "Please excuse me."

Then he hurried away.

Mrs. Moon watched the deacon retreat. "Doesn't that man ever knock?" she asked.

Rev. Camden shrugged.

"I'll walk you out," he said.

The school parking lot was practically empty. Lucy leaned against a tree and stared into the distance.

At the other end of the parking lot, near a green area everyone called the Park, Lucy saw Jimmy Moon. He was walking with two punks.

Her heart skipped a beat.

Justin Dade!

Lucy stepped into the shadows and watched as the boys went into the Park.

She took a deep breath and looked around. There was still no sign of Mary. Then she looked back toward the Park. Justin and Jimmy definitely seemed to be up to something.

Lucy walked toward the Park.

At that moment, Rev. Camden pulled into the parking lot and stopped the car. He climbed out and looked around. No Lucy.

Then he saw her. She was walking toward the Park. He was about to call her when he spotted Jimmy Moon.

Lucy entered the Park in time to see Jimmy exchange a wad of money with Justin for a plastic bag of something. The third kid stood a few feet away, acting as lookout.

Lucy moved toward them. Jimmy saw her coming. So did Justin, who sneered and said something to Jimmy.

Then Lucy heard the squeal of tires. As if by magic, she and the boys were suddenly surrounded. Men were coming from everywhere, and all of them were shouting and pointing guns.

"Freeze!" one of them shouted.

"Down on your knees," another man cried. He grabbed Justin by the scruff of his neck and threw the boy to the ground.

"Don't move," the man commanded, resting the muzzle of his gun behind Justin's ear as he cuffed him.

As another man wrestled the lookout to the grass, Jimmy stood speechless, staring at Lucy. Finally, he was pushed to the ground and handcuffed.

"Get down!" a voice cried in Lucy's ear. "I'm talking to you, sister!"

Lucy jumped, startled, and tried to turn around. Strong hands grabbed her shoulders as her feet were literally kicked out from under her. Lucy was lowered to the ground gently but firmly.

Before she realized what was happening, she felt cold metal handcuffs around her wrists.

Lucy didn't struggle. But she did look up—straight into the eyes of Jimmy Moon.

Jimmy turned away, a look of guilt on his tortured face.

As Rev. Camden raced across the parking lot, an unmarked police car shot past him. The vehicle skidded to a halt on the edge of the Park, and three detectives jumped out and ran toward the grass.

Rev. Camden tried to get to Lucy, but a policeman intercepted him.

"You can't go in there, Reverend!" he cried.

"My daughter's in there!" Rev. Camden said.

The man blinked. "I hope you're wrong," the man said. "Because if your daughter is in there, then she's under arrest for narcotics trafficking."

The Camden house was tense that evening. Everyone knew a crisis of some kind had occurred and that Lucy was involved. But Mrs. Camden had refused to answer any of Mary's questions until her husband could speak with all of them, as a family.

Restless, Mary decided to check up on Simon, who, she knew, was probably still angry with her.

She found him lying on the bed, reading a schoolbook.

Mary smiled. "So, are you talking to me?"

Simon looked up. His eyes were flashing. "I don't know," he replied. "Did you talk to my coach? Am I still the lowly equipment manager?"

"Yes to both," Mary answered. "And I'm sorry, all right?"

She sat down on the edge of the bed. "It was my fault," she continued. "I shouldn't have opened my big mouth. You were right. You were going to make the team, and I blew it for you."

She reached out and put a hand on Simon's shoulder. "You're a good ballplayer, Simon. Your coach said so."

"I was going to make the team," he said slowly. "But was I good enough to make catcher?"

"Sure!" Mary lied.

"The coach didn't really say that, did he?" Simon said accusingly. "You're making it up!"

Mary was silent.

"What did the coach really say?" Simon asked.

"He said it was a tough decision," Mary said, trying to soften the blow. "But that in all fairness, you weren't quite ready."

Simon thought about it. "Okay," he said at last. "I can take the truth."

"All right, then," Mary said. "This is the truth, too. The coach said you can still work out with the team. And you should."

Simon's eyes lit up. "Even batting practice?"

"I guess," Mary replied. "He also said that if anyone drops out, you're on. That's one reason why he picked you as equipment manager."

"Wow!" Simon cried.

"And even if no one drops out, if you and I practice together really hard, I'm sure you'll make the team next year, okay?"

"You'll see," Simon vowed. "I'm going to be the best darn equipment manager anyone's ever seen."

"Great!" Mary said. "And you and I will practice every week."

Simon looked at his sister. "Can I bring a friend along, too?" he asked. "Mike's a really great guy, and he's good, too. He just needs to learn a few moves."

"Mike?" Mary said. "Mike Hensleigh?"

"Yeah, that's him," Simon replied. "How did you know?"

"Isn't he the guy who made catcher?" Mary studied her brother.

Simon nodded.

"And you're going to help him?"

Simon nodded again.

"Sure," Mary said with a smile. "Bring Mike along. I'd be honored to coach you both."

* * *

Later that night, after the twins were asleep, Rev. and Mrs. Camden sat down in the kitchen with Lucy.

"I know I'm in for some heavy lecturing, and I deserve it," Lucy began. She looked at her father.

"Yes, I think you're right," he said.

"Before you start, is it okay if I say something first?"

Her parents both nodded.

Lucy took a deep breath.

"After tonight, we should never talk about Jimmy Moon again," she said. "But I know the whole story now, and I want to tell you what really happened."

She paused. "A couple of months ago, Jimmy got busted when some friends talked him into trying out some drugs. The cops came, and everybody scattered and Jimmy was the only one caught.

"He was left holding the evidence, so Jimmy made a deal.

"I can't say what kind of deal, but since you're both smarter than I am, you probably already realized what Jimmy was up to and that's why you told me to stay away from him."

Tears sprang up in Lucy's eyes. "So you were right and I was wrong," she concluded. "I could have gotten hurt today, but I didn't."

Lucy's voice was unsteady.

"I sampled being a grown-up today, and I didn't like it. I'll take it when the time comes. But until then, I'm going to be comfortable knowing as much as you guys want to tell me."

Lucy turned to her mom. "If you want to join Dad at church this Sunday, I'd like to stay home and practice some of my nurturing on my little brothers."

She waited for her parents' response. Rev. Camden spoke first.

"That's even better than the lecture I was going to give," he declared.

Mrs. Camden smiled proudly at her daughter. "She's going to make a very good mother someday."

Lucy hugged them both.

In the foyer, the front door swung open, surprising Mary.

"Hey, you two!" she said when Matt came in, carrying Ruthie over his shoulder. Ruthie looked like she was sleeping after her big afternoon with Matt.

"Hey, Mary," Matt replied.

"You missed all the excitement," Mary said.

"Oh?" Matt said, raising an eyebrow. "Like what?"

"Oh, nothing," Mary cooed. "Just Lucy getting arrested for narcotics trafficking."

"Yeah, right," Matt said.

Ruthie stirred. "I love you, Matt," she whispered between yawns.

"I love you, too," Matt said. He carried his little sister upstairs to bed.

TEN

Matt picked up Shana at eight o'clock sharp.

He drove them both to an outdoor concert in the park. He spread out a blanket near a gazebo and produced a basket of food and cans of soda.

The two of them ate and laughed and talked until the concert began. Arms around each other, they listened to the beautiful music as it echoed across the grass. The night was clear and the stars were brilliant.

When the concert ended, Matt gathered up their stuff. It was still early, so he took Shana to a lookout on top of a hill.

Matt spread the blanket on the hood of his car. The night was chilly, so Matt and

Shana huddled together and gazed up at the stars.

"This was a wonderful evening," Shana sighed. "The music, the food—and, of course, the company."

She looked at Matt and smiled. He reached out and took her hand.

Then Matt told Shana everything.

He told her about the apartment and about Connie. He told her about his confrontation with Charlotte and the scene at Crawford College.

"I just wanted to have my own place," Matt explained. "I wanted you to be able to come to *my* place—not my parents'."

"I knew you were upset the night we had that fight," Matt said. "And I didn't want us to ever fight again. So I tried to fix the problem."

"I'm glad you told me the truth," Shana said. "I'd heard some things that bothered me."

"Why didn't you ask me about it?" Matt asked.

"Because I trust you," Shana replied. "You've always been honest with me."

Matt smiled. "My dad always says that honesty is the best policy," he told her.

Shana leaned over and kissed him. "I'm

lucky to have you," she said.

Matt shook his head. "No," he insisted. "*I'm* the lucky one."

"Let's just say we're both lucky," Shana said. "And leave it at that."

The Camdens rose early the next morning. Since Lucy had agreed to take care of the twins while the family was at church, her mother handed her a list of emergency phone numbers.

"Thanks, Mom," Lucy said. "But I don't think I'll be needing the veterinarian's phone number. I'm sure Happy will be fine."

"You can't be too careful," Mrs. Camden cautioned.

"Have fun today," Lucy said with a glance at her father. Then she leaned closer and whispered to her mother, "I don't think Dad suspects a thing."

Mrs. Camden chuckled. "He suspects *something*," she replied. "But not what's coming."

As Rev. Camden prepared for church services, he felt like a condemned prisoner.

As he donned his robes, he decided that this would be his last chance to face his congregation with dignity.

They can fire me if they want, he thought. *But they're going to hear my sermon first.*

When the organ began to play, Rev. Camden grabbed his notes and his Bible. Then he took a deep breath and walked to the pulpit.

Rev. Camden saw his family lined up in the front pew. He had mixed feelings about their presence. He was grateful for their support. But he was not happy they were there to see his humiliating dismissal.

Forty-five minutes later, Rev. Camden was finishing up what he was sure would be the last sermon he would give in Glenoak.

He was happy with the way his sermon had been received—until he reached his closing remarks.

"And so, we can never give up the struggle to learn. Even though we find ourselves completely in the dark, with no idea what is really going on…"

Rev. Camden heard giggling in the church. He ignored it and pressed on.

"I suppose it's our need to control things in our lives that makes us want to know more than is available to us. Our thoughts often run to the worst possible scenario because we don't trust that we will be taken care of."

Rev. Camden looked up. His eyes met his wife's. She was smiling brightly. *A little too brightly*, he thought. She looked as if she would soon burst into peals of laughter.

"But when you think about it," Rev. Camden continued, "we've always been taken care of, from the day we were born…"

He gazed out at the crowd. The congregation was shifting impatiently.

"So we must ask ourselves. What is the point of all this…this paranoia that something terrible is about to happen?"

The laughter grew louder. Rev. Camden looked around the church. The laughter died quickly.

He returned to his notes and realized he'd lost his place.

Suddenly, the door at the back of the church opened and an elderly man wearing a clerical robe identical to Rev. Camden's stepped into the room.

Rev. Camden blinked as the man strode boldly up to the pulpit. Confused, he looked at his wife. She was actually laughing.

The elderly minister smiled. "Forgive

me for interrupting, Reverend Camden," he said. "But I just couldn't go on watching a fellow preacher's sermon getting laughs in all the wrong places."

Everyone burst into laughter.

Then the stranger waved them to silence. He spoke in a loud, clear voice that didn't need a microphone.

"To all newcomers, allow me to introduce myself." He turned to Rev. Camden and thrust out his hand.

"I'm Doctor Bergen—the Reverend Bergen, as I was known when I was the minister of this church," he declared.

Rev. Camden's mouth gaped in surprise. "You're Reverend Bergen?" he stammered. "We've never met. There was an interim minister when I was brought in. But..."

Rev. Camden's voice trailed off in confusion. Laughter erupted once again.

"But what am I doing here?" Reverend Bergen said, smiling.

"Allow me to say that you yourself had every right to be paranoid this week," Rev. Bergen said. "And don't try to deny it," he added quickly. "I got a full report from almost every person in this congregation—including Mrs. Camden."

Rev. Camden looked at his family. He could tell they had all been in on it. Even Lucy, who had volunteered to stay at home so Mrs. Camden could attend church this morning.

Rev. Camden turned beet red.

"Because your congregation, your deacons, and everyone in this church—even your family—have been scheming…"

Rev. Bergen turned to Rev. Camden with a mischievous twinkle in his eyes.

"This Sunday marks your twentieth year at Glenoak," Rev. Bergen continued. "So, happy anniversary!"

The congregation leapt to their feet and began to applaud. The clapping went on for quite a while, until Rev. Camden was so overwhelmed that he wanted to cry—as undignified as that might be.

"I hate to cut your sermon short," Rev. Bergen added. "But there is a potluck lunch and special ice-cream cake for everyone in the recreation room, in your honor."

Rev. Camden shook the elderly minister's hand again, then faced his flock and bowed.

"God bless you for twenty years of fine service. May you have twenty years more," Rev. Bergen said. "And who knows?" he added. "Maybe someday you'll be invited back so you can interrupt the man who takes *your* job."

The congregation cheered. Lou and Sid rushed to congratulate Rev. Camden.

"I'll get you for this, Lou!" Rev. Camden cried.

The deacon laughed. "Sorry about barging into your office all week, Eric," he explained. "I kept needing to check your answering machine to see about the desk being delivered."

Rev. Camden turned to Reverend Bergen. "Oh, yes," he said. "About the desk..."

"It's the very one I used when I was minister here," the elderly man explained. "It's my gift to you. I figured it missed the place."

Rev. Camden smiled and patted his predecessor's shoulder. "And I think, judging by the response to your appearance this morning, that everyone in this place misses *you*, Reverend Bergen."

"You're a fine replacement," the reverend replied. "I couldn't have done better myself. I know my flock is in good hands, Rev. Camden."

Rev. Camden lowered his eyes humbly.

"Thank you, Reverend Bergen," he said sincerely. "You don't know how much that means to me."

Then Rev. Camden's whole family rushed up to him and gave him big hugs.

Matt shook his father's hand. "I'm proud to be your son."

"You're the greatest, Dad," Simon added.

Mrs. Camden touched her husband's arm. "It was so hard watching you suffer all week," she said.

Rev. Camden grinned. "You loved every minute of it," he said, giving her a kiss.

As their lips met, Rev. Camden silently gave a special thanks for his most precious gift of all.

His family.

MARY'S STORY

Big sis Mary seems to have it all together: She's practical, super-smart, beautiful, vivacious, and a rising star on her school's basketball team. But beneath her perfect exterior, sixteen-year-old Mary is struggling to figure out boys, friends, parents, and life in general—not to mention her younger sister Lucy!

Available wherever books are sold!
ISBN: 0-375-80332-7

And coming January 2000:
Rivals
ISBN: 0-375-80337-8

Mr. Nice Guy
ISBN: 0-375-80338-6

Middle Sister
ISBN: 0-375-80336-X